NIGHT STALKER

Paula Beaty

Paranormal Romantic Suspense

New Concepts   Georgia

Be sure to check out our website for the very best in fiction at fantastic prices!

When you visit our webpage, you can:
* Read excerpts of currently available books
* View cover art of upcoming books and current releases
* Find out more about the talented artists who capture the magic of the writer's imagination on the covers
* Order books from our backlist
* Find out the latest NCP and author news--including any upcoming book signings by your favorite NCP author
* Read author bios and reviews of our books
* Get NCP submission guidelines
* And so much more!

We offer a 20% discount on all new Trade Paperback releases ordered from our website!

Be sure to visit our webpage to find the best deals in e-books and paperbacks! To find out about our new releases as soon as they are available, please be sure to sign up for our newsletter (http://www.newconceptspublishing.com/newsletter.htm) or join our reader group (http://groups.yahoo.com/group/new_concepts_pub/join)!

The newsletter is available by double opt in only and our customer information is *never* shared!

Visit our webpage at:
www.newconceptspublishing.com

Night Stalker is an original publication of NCP. This work has never before appeared in book form. This work is a novel. Any similarity to actual persons or events is purely coincidental.

New Concepts Publishing, Inc.
5202 Humphreys Rd.
Lake Park, GA 31636

ISBN 1-58608-745-2
2006 © Paula Beaty
Cover art (c) copyright 2006 Kat Richards

NCP books are available at special quantity discounts for bulk purchases for sales promotions, premiums, fund raising, or educational use. For details, write, email, or phone New Concepts Publishing, Inc., 5202 Humphreys Rd., Lake Park, GA 31636; Ph. 229-257-0367, Fax 229-219-1097; orders@newconceptspublishing.com.

First NCP Trade Paperback Printing: March 2006

Chapter One

She felt his hot breath sticky on her neck, smelled the rancid stench emanating from him. Her skin crawled as his hands slid over her body. Nausea rolled through her belly.

"Take anything you want, just please don't hurt me." She whispered her plea, forcing the words over the terror, but he made no sign that he heard her. Bending down, he trailed his tongue from her jawbone up her right cheek to the tear at the corner of her tightly squeezed eye.

The knife in his hand glistened overhead. It was too late to scream. He plunged the knife deep into her chest, piercing her lung and making it impossible for her to cry out for help. She felt the life drain from her body.

Soon she floated high above the man, staring down at the beautiful face of a woman, a face that wasn't the one she saw in the mirror every day.

Taylor wanted to scream, to run from the scene before her, but she knew it was impossible. The only way out was to go forward. To focus on what her eyes were seeing. To find some detail to help nail this piece of scum. She watched in horror as he drew the knife out of the woman's body and wiped the blood down the length of her torso. Taylor cringed in horror.

"Take the mask off and let me see your face, you lunatic!"

Willing him to listen, to hear her, she yelled again. This time louder. Anger and fear seared through her at the wasted effort. It was useless. He couldn't hear her. She really didn't know how much more of this she could take.

The killer untied his victim's hands from the headboard and placed them over the bloody pool marring her chest. Taking a single red rose out of his sweatshirt pocket, he threaded it through her limp fingers.

Taylor wanted this sick maniac behind bars, so she tried to burn into her memory everything she could. His blurred image gave her the impression that he was around six feet tall, maybe two hundred and fifty pounds, and dressed completely in black from his black ski mask to his leather gloves. He seemed like an angel of death. For all that this vision showed Taylor, it still wasn't enough to go on. It wasn't enough to catch him before he killed again.

The freak always whispered, making it hard to pinpoint an accent or speech impediment, anything to give the police a lead. No fingerprints were ever found and since he didn't rape his victims, no DNA samples were found either. He was meticulous, a murderer prepared for anything, and Taylor was at a loss as to what to do next. Fear settled like a lead brick in the bottom of her stomach. She couldn't shake the feeling that she recognized this victim.

Leaning over his victim, he whispered in the young woman's ear, "Sweet Evita, you were too lovely for this world to bear. Please forgive me."

It was always the same thing. He always said they were too lovely for this world to bear. He always asked for forgiveness. What did it mean? If only she could figure it out so no one else would have to die.

He rose from the bedside and began to look around the room. This was different. Had he dropped something? He turned and looked up at Taylor. Usually he disappeared into the night without a trace. This time though, he stood and stared right at her. He couldn't hear her and had never acknowledged that he was aware of her presence in any way. But now he was looking right at her. *Can he see me?* Taylor felt a chill run through her as the thought took hold.

He reached out a gloved hand towards her just as a loud bang pulled her from her dream, followed by the smooth, silky voice of her sister Lana calling out her name.

She jerked awake and stared into the worried eyes of her sister, brown, soulful eyes that were filled with fear. "It happened again, didn't it?" Lana placed a cold rag on her forehead. "He struck again?"

Taylor nodded. Tears were streaming down her cheeks at the thought that another woman's life had ended because this lunatic was still free. She hadn't asked for these visions, and most days she sure wished that whoever gave them to her would take them back.

Taylor allowed herself to be wrapped up in the loving arms of her older sister. These dreams took so much out of her. Ever since this crazy person had started killing young women, Taylor's life had been plagued with nightmares of terror and death.

Taylor found control again, her sobbing subsiding enough for Lana to release her and grab a pad and pen from the end table. Lana made herself comfortable on the matching sofa across from the tan leather recliner Taylor huddled in.

"Okay, give it to me straight. What happened this time, did you see any clues as to who this guy could be?" Lana seemed to wait with bated breath, her pen poised over the pad of paper.

Taylor pulled in a deep cleansing breath, squared her shoulders, and recited every detail she could recall about the scene that had played out before her, even mentioning that she had a fleeting notion that she might know the young lady. Her voice came out as a monotone, as if she were reading the instructions to setting up a stereo system.

She left out the part about the killer noticing her there, reaching for her. Taylor needed to mull over those details before scaring her big sister. What could it all mean?

"Taylor ... Taylor, are you okay?" Her sister's strained voice floated through the air.

What she wouldn't give for a full night's rest. With no nightmares.

Dragging her hands through her tangled, mousy brown curls, Taylor blew out an exasperated breath. "I'm fine. I just, well, to tell the truth I'm exhausted. Even the sleeping pills don't stop the dreams long enough anymore." She met her sister's worried gaze.

Lana gave a quick nod and stated encouragingly, "We'll beat it, sis. We'll figure it out, and then you can sleep for a week if you want. I promise."

Taylor barely managed to smile at her sister's attempts to help. She knew it was a promise that couldn't be kept. If not this crime, then it would be something else. She wondered exactly how long it would take for her to go as crazy as the criminals in her visions. A few more months of little to no sleep ought to do it.

Her life had been normal up until eight months ago when a hit-and-run accident left her in a coma for two weeks. Before that, she'd had a boyfriend and friends who considered her one of the sanest people they knew. Now she was the crazy woman in apartment 2B.

Her boyfriend, Tommy, deserted her a month after she came out of the coma when she first started having these "dreams."

The vividness of the visions frightened Taylor at first, but the dreams were harmless, just brutal to her peace of mind. They were haunting images of a girl being abducted from a playground or of vicious pit bulls mauling an older woman out for an evening jog.

When the newspapers later depicted exactly what she saw in her visions, she approached the police with what she knew. They, of course, had looked at her like she had grown a second head on her shoulders. That was when Tommy said he "needed some alone time, but he still wanted to be friends." *Yeah, that had happened!* He took off for parts unknown and didn't even bother leaving a forwarding address.

Gradually, the police began to believe her. They even came to her for information she might have concerning any other crimes. She'd been proud to assist in bringing two young girls home safe after being kidnapped from the school bus stop.

The police agreed never to mention her involvement to the families or reporters. Taylor didn't want to be labeled a head case, but something obviously leaked out to her neighbors, because they avoided her like the plague.

Even Lana had thought her a little crazy at first, but eventually she came around. They'd only had each other since their parents' deaths. If not for Lana, Taylor didn't know if she would have made it through these last few months.

* * * *

Closing her tired eyes, Taylor rested her head against the bath pillow. Trying to remember her life before the powers-that-be slapped her with the crazy lady label proved harder and harder each day. She used to have a good job that she liked--well okay, she tolerated--but it was a regular job. She had led a normal life.

Now it was all she could do to make it through the day without losing her lunch because of these bloody visions. Thankfully their parents had left them with more than enough money to make a comfortable life for themselves, but that didn't mean she wanted to stop working. Keeping busy was the way to enjoy life, not being locked up in some apartment.

Unable to stay awake at work, she eventually quit her job as an administrative assistant at a very prestigious advertising firm. The dreams had never publicly embarrassed her, thankfully, but her boss constantly eyed her suspiciously. With the accident coming only a few months after losing her parents in a house fire, he politely suggested that she take some time off.

Could life possibly get any worse?

Lana barged into the bathroom and plopped herself down on the toilet seat. "I called Richard and told him about these new visions. He said he'd get the detective assigned to the case to meet us at the café in two hours."

Taylor groaned as she took in what her sister had just said. Just wonderful. Now she'd have to prove herself to another skeptic.

As it turned out life could get worse.

Richard Blanchard was a great detective and had become a wonderful friend in the past few months. He believed her, but he worked in the Missing Persons Division. Taylor hated the fact that he wouldn't be able to work with her this time. She knew there would be another attack soon. They didn't have the time to convince someone else of her ability. The killer still ran loose. Too many women had died already.

Taylor merely smiled up at her sister, snuggled down farther into her warm bubble bath and stated as cheerfully as she could, "Thanks for handling everything for me, Lana."

Lana waved off her gratitude. "Hey, that's what big sisters

are for. Besides, I can't get enough of Richard. He's a hunk and a half." She fanned herself in that innocent, southern-belle-with-the-vapors way.

Taylor laughed at her sister's antics. "Hey you, leave poor, sweet Richard alone. I think he has a girlfriend anyway." Something akin to fear passed over her sister's face. That couldn't be right though, Lana wasn't afraid of anything, so Taylor ignored the tingle of suspicion.

"Really, how can you be sure?"

"Oh, it was just something he said the last time we talked. It sounded like it's pretty serious, so don't you go making plays for him." She shook her finger at her sister as if she was a mother scolding a young child. "I will not have a home wrecker for a sister."

Lana looked taken aback. "Me, a home wrecker? Whatever do you mean, sister dear?"

Taylor just splashed water at her and gave a stern look. "Don't make me have to take you over my knee, young lady."

They both burst out laughing when they realized Taylor sounded just like their mother that time they had done some not-so-nice things to the neighbor's cat when they were young girls playing dress-up.

Lana left Taylor to finish her bath. A warm bubble bath always helped relax the tense muscles she had after a vision. She loved relaxing in the big garden tub. A few lavender-scented candles, some soft music and she could probably drift right off to sleep. But it was dangerous to fall asleep in the bathtub, so she resigned herself to just having relaxed muscles. Sleep would have to come later. Climbing out, she pulled the plug and wrapped herself in her pink terry cloth robe.

Grabbing the towel off the rack, she wrapped it around

her hair and headed for her room. Better try and make herself more presentable. She was bound to be under extreme scrutiny when she met the homicide detective.

Taylor had the fleeting vision of herself wearing her gypsy dress from a few Halloweens back to meet the man who would most definitely be looking at her like she belonged in a mental hospital. She eyed it up and down skeptically before deciding on just a comfortable pair of jeans and her 'Have a nice day!' T-shirt. No need to scare off the poor guy before she revealed the extent of her abilities.

* * * *

Taylor and Lana sat across from Richard and Detective Cade Wills in a booth at Marge's Café down the street from their apartment complex. If only this were a double date.

Marge's was a great little hole in the wall Taylor loved. The sixties diner meets Planet Hollywood theme suited her perfectly. The black and white checkered vinyl floor, dark pink bar stools, and the disco ball hanging from the ceiling always made her smile. Hand-drawn pictures of Hollywood stars adorned every inch of wall possible and each table had its own small working jukebox. It might not be the most fancy of restaurants, but the food was good and the people were extremely friendly.

The perfect place for a first date, if this were one.

Both of the men sitting across from them were handsome. Richard reminded Taylor of a brawny barbarian. He wore his shoulder-length, sandy blond hair pulled back in a ponytail, and he never grew an actual beard, but always seemed to have a five o'clock shadow. He was tall, broad shouldered, with narrow hips, strong legs and he packed a gun, which upped his dangerous bad-boy image loads. On top of all that, he was actually a very nice guy.

Upon inspection of Detective Wills, Taylor decided he definitely qualified for her hot and juicy award. He had short brown hair and piercing blue-green eyes and stood a few inches taller than her five-foot-four frame. He was not quite as muscular as Richard, but just as imposing. He made his presence felt in the room, which was apparent by all the females turning to glance and smile his way. Taylor gave him brownie points for ignoring the stares and giggles.

Richard had learned to trust her after all these months of working closely together to find missing kids, but Cade was meeting her for the first time. His lack of enthusiasm clearly stated he could find something better to do with his time. Taylor prepared herself for the usual lack of trust and skepticism.

"So Richard tells me that you've been having, um ... visions ... of my murder victims." Taylor held his scrutinizing gaze even though every muscle in her body was screaming for her to look away. He seemed almost eager to hear what she had to say.

She took a bite of the barely touched hamburger she'd ordered, chewed slowly, mentally counting to ten. She plastered on her best smile and replied, "Yes, I've had *visions* of the women that were killed. Seven, to be exact. Is there something you'd like me to tell you that wasn't released to the press, Detective Wills?"

After being doubted so much in the past it was hard not to be defensive when discussing her visions. She didn't want to fight with the yummy detective; she wanted to solve these murders so no one else had to lose a loved one and maybe, just maybe, she could live a normal life.

Lana placed a hand on Taylor's arm and gave a gentle

squeeze. She was glad for the extra support. Between the lack of sleep and her hormones going stir crazy at the nearness of so much wonderful smelling male essence, she was feeling completely drained. She didn't think she could take being looked down upon like she was the sideshow freak at some traveling carnival anymore.

She felt Detective Wills' stare all the way down to her toes as he considered her question. She hoped he didn't notice the dark circles under her eyes. His blue-green eyes gave away no clues as to what he was thinking.

Impatience resonated in his words as he said, "Okay Ms. Cole, why don't you tell me something that no one outside of my department should know."

When her smile disappeared, a small smile appeared on his gorgeous face. Heat crept up her neck, but it wasn't from embarrassment. Was that attraction she felt? No way. It couldn't be ... could it? She shook her head. That grin meant he thought he had her stumped.

Her grin matched his as she silently enjoyed the fact that she was going to be able to provide him with an answer that would prove she wasn't some head case. She whispered, "He places their hands over their wounds and gives them a rose to hold."

Cade's eyes became almost as big as the platter in front him that held his untouched hamburger. He stuttered, "I ... I, yes, that's right. How did you know that?"

Richard slapped Cade on the back and disintegrated into a fit of laughter. Cade looked from Richard, who could barely contain his laughter, to a smiling Lana, then finally came to rest on Taylor. His jaw worked up and down. Their eyes locked and Taylor felt her heart do a somersault. She was right, his eyes told her so.

When Richard's laughter finally died down, Taylor

continued, "He breaks in while they're sleeping, ties their hands to the headboard, cuts their clothes off, then when they awaken he licks..." A light bulb sizzled to life in her head. "Oh my gosh. DNA!" Taylor suddenly had the urge to dance naked on the table. She had it, it had been niggling her in the back of her mind this whole time and now bam! there it was.

"What do you mean, DNA? He licks what?" Cade nearly came out of his seat.

Taylor turned to Lana, gripping her hands tightly as she began bouncing in the booth. She felt herself beaming with discovery. "I did it, Lana. I got him!" Turning back to face Cade and Richard, she blurted out, "He licks his victims' cheeks!"

Several customers' heads turned to observe the outburst.

"Well, Ms. Cole, that could be an important piece of information. If it's true. I'll get with my Captain on that." Detective Wills shook his head. "Wait Ms. Cole, earlier you said seven victims? There have only been six bodies found."

The smile slipped from Taylor's face. All the joy rushed from her just as quickly as it had appeared. "I'm sorry, but you'll find another one. Her name is Evita."

Cade opened his mouth to speak, but was cut off by the ringing of his cell phone. Taylor watched as he muttered an apology then grabbed his phone from the holster on his hip and flipped it open, barking, "Detective Wills."

Taylor watched the play of emotion on his face as his eyes clouded over and became unreadable. "What was her name?" He blew out a long breath and raked his hand through his hair. "Damn. Okay, I'll be there in ten minutes." Closing the phone and placing it back in his hip holster, he looked hard at Taylor.

"They found her."

Those three words rocked her to the core, but nothing prepared her for what he was about to say.

"She lived in your apartment building, Ms. Cole." Suspicion colored Cade's words.

Taylor felt the bottom fall out of her stomach. Someone had been murdered in her apartment building. She couldn't recall any of her neighbors being named Evita.

Time was a blur until they pulled up in front of her building. When Taylor saw the police cars and yellow crime scene tape, she knew he'd been right. She held tight to Lana's hand as the detectives led them inside.

Richard tried his best to assure them everything would be okay, but nothing penetrated the loud humming noise echoing through Taylor's ears. The victim's apartment was right next door to hers.

Her stomach lurched.

She whispered, "Consuela." She'd been wrong. How could she have been wrong about the name?

Lana gasped loudly, and Cade told her to wait outside with Richard.

When Cade grabbed her hand, Taylor was suddenly surrounded in warmth. Cade's strength snaked through her giving her the nerve to continue into the apartment. She was almost inclined to let go, but held on for dear life, knowing that she might need the support since she'd never seen a real dead body up close and personal before.

Cade flashed his badge to the officer standing at the front door, who lifted the yellow crime scene tape to allow them access. They ducked under and Cade squeezed her hand while asking if she would be able to recognize the body from her vision. Her brows drew together in confusion, because he already knew who it was, but nodded her assent. Taylor drew upon Cade's silent strength and was suddenly glad that he was there with her.

They walked past several police officers snapping pictures of the apartment and putting things in big plastic bags. When she stepped into the bedroom, the smell of death hit her hard. She placed a hand over her mouth to keep what little she had eaten of her lunch down. Cade pulled a blue and white plaid handkerchief from his pocket and handed it to her. She immediately placed the handkerchief over her mouth and nose, breathing in a distinctively male scent.

"Are you okay to do this, Ms. Cole?" Cade grasped her shoulders and began to turn her away from the bed.

"I'm fine." Taylor's muffled reply seemed to echo throughout the room.

When she finally appeared to have a hold of her emotions, she stepped forward to see the body on the bed. Consuela's pale, lifeless body lay just as the killer had left her. Her hands were folded across the wound Taylor knew lay beneath. The red rosebud clasped between her fingers served as a reminder of the devastation that had ended her quiet neighbor's life. Her comforter lay crumpled in a heap by the foot of the bed.

Except for the people snapping photographs, everything was as Taylor had seen in her vision. Each detail she'd tried so hard to remember. Everything. Except....

"That wasn't in my vision." Taylor pointed to the words written in what appeared to be blood on the wall above her neighbor's bed.

Cade read them aloud, "'I see you.' What the hell does that mean? He's never written anything before."

He was definitely confused, but Taylor knew exactly what it meant. The killer *had* seen her. She hadn't imagined it. He knew she had seen what he'd done. *Oh God!* In a panic she turned and fled the room.

Taylor darted out of the apartment, dodging police officers left and right and sped out the door, past Richard and Lana. She vaguely heard them calling her name, but she couldn't stop. She had to reach the comfort and safety of her own home. She unlocked her door and flung it wide with a loud resounding bang, then sprinted towards the bathroom. Finally, she did what she'd wanted to do for the last hour ... she lost her lunch.

She felt Lana's hands pulling her mass of unruly curls out of her face and heard her whisper soothing words. A cool wet rag was placed on her neck to help cool her body temperature.

Taylor hated that her sister had to see her like this. Hell, she hated that the detectives had to see her like this, but she was helpless to stop the nausea that flowed through her.

He knew I was there!

How is that possible?

* * * *

Cade tapped Richard's shoulder and motioned for him to follow him out of the room. Once they reached the living room and were far enough out of earshot of the women, he turned on Richard. "She knows something!"

"She told you what she knows." Richard placed his hands on his hips and took the defensive stance that Cade had come to know meant his friend wasn't budging an inch.

"He wrote something on the wall this time, Richard, and she knows what it means. I saw her eyes. She knew!" Cade started pacing the length of the living room. "Why would he break his *modus operandi*?"

"I..." Richard started to speak, but stopped when Lana entered the room.

"She's taken one of her sleeping pills, Detective Wills, so if you want to question her it will have to be later. She'll be out like a light in no time." Lana crossed her arms over her chest.

Cade's frustration grew with this new turn of events. He had to get home. "Have her call me the minute she wakes up. I need answers, Ms. Cole, and I aim to get them." He left the apartment and silently shut the door behind him.

* * * *

Taylor peeked through the crack of her bedroom door. She wanted to help out in any way possible to solve this case, but she was completely terrified at the moment.

Richard said, "I'm sorry about that, Lana. He is a very good detective, it's just..."

"It's just that he has a murder investigation to work. I totally got it. But Taylor has to deal with this too. He needs to realize that." Lana stared at the business card as if she was tempted to tear it up. Thinking better of it, she jammed it into her front jean pocket.

Taylor shut the door quietly and crossed to her bed. She lay awake staring at the numbers on the alarm clock as they slowly ticked by. She'd been so scared when she thought he'd seen her. Knowing that he actually saw her had her insides twisted in knots. No one ever acknowledged her when she was in a vision. It had always been like she was watching a movie, an observer to it all.

She knew that Lana lied to the detective about her being asleep, but she really needed to be alone right now to sort out the visions, the Night Stalker and the strange attraction she was experiencing towards Cade Wills. When he'd squeezed her hand earlier, she had the brief thought of how nice it would be to pretend he was holding her hand for reasons other than assuring her that looking at a dead body would be okay.

Taylor had never seen a dead body. Her parents had died in a fire so the funeral was closed casket. She remembered wishing they'd died differently so she could see their beautiful faces once more. Now all she had were memories and photos.

Consuela had been a good person, always friendly and smiling. She was a good neighbor, and now she was dead.

Why did she have to die? Why did any of them have to die?

The faint sounds of Lana moving around the apartment doing her usual busywork reached Taylor's ears. Lana never allowed the house to be messy, but when she was nervous or upset, she always found something to do. Taylor wished that her sister could have a life. She didn't want to have to be taken care of by Lana forever.

The effects of the sleeping pills started to claim her. Closing her eyes, she prayed for a dreamless sleep, but instinctively knew it wouldn't come.

* * * *

Taylor inhaled deeply, catching the fragrant spring breeze. The birds could be heard chirping somewhere farther down the path. The sky was a light blue with scattered clouds. The sounds of laughter coming from the children on the playground drifted to her. It felt peaceful just to sit in the park listening to the sounds of nature, reading a wonderful romance novel.

She wished she could stay in the park all afternoon, but she needed to get back to work. She hated the fact that they didn't own a car and she hated riding the Metro bus even more, but it saved her and Lana money in the long run.

She felt the bump as the men passed by her, knocking her book out of her hands and right into the street. Stepping off

*the curb to retrieve it, an intense pain shot through her
body as the beat up Buick plowed into her. Her head hit the
windshield, then she rolled completely over the length of
the car, finally coming to land on the concrete a few
seconds later.*

*Taylor heard the shouts and screams as people rushed to
her side. Sirens rang in the distance. Then silence loomed
and she felt extreme peace.*

*Seconds later a man was beside her and she smiled up at
him, ready to thank him for his help. It struck her as odd
that someone would be wearing a ski mask on such a
beautiful day. She emitted a loud, piercing scream as his
face faded into the background.*

*The evil look in his piercing ice blue eyes and the small
smirk that she saw through the mouth hole of the ski mask
would remain forever embedded in her mind.*

Taylor woke up screaming and clutching the blankets to
her chest. Lana was already there with a wet wash rag and
her always present understanding. She waited patiently
while Taylor got herself under control and then Taylor told
her everything about her dream. Even though Taylor was
exhausted, she couldn't make herself relax enough to go
back to sleep so while Lana dozed on the couch, she stayed
up reading.

Chapter Two

After such a long night, they felt the need to do something to get their blood pumping the next morning. Making the decision that a short jog would do just that, they quickly changed into their sweats and headed out for a nice run in the park.

Taylor's eyes immediately caught on the yellow crime scene tape that remained across her neighbor's door. The fear and sorrow came back full force. Her heart ached for the families that lost their loved ones to this murderer. She felt a strong tug on her hand as Lana whispered words of encouragement.

"It'll be all right, sis. They'll catch him."

Taylor looked from the door to her sister and back again. "I just don't understand why he called her Evita. He's never messed up on their names before. He knows them. I just haven't figured out the connection yet. But I know he knows them."

"I'm sure Detective Overly Rude and Overbearing will make the connection and catch this guy." Taylor let Lana lead her down the stairs and out of the building. "Richard says he's a very good detective. One of the youngest homicide detectives ever. He solved some homicide case while he was a beat cop or some such nonsense."

Taylor remembered briefly thinking that he didn't seem to be old enough to be a homicide detective. Cade must be good or they wouldn't have assigned him to such a high profile case. She could only hope he would believe her and work with her to solve these killings.

The jog around the park helped clear her head. Her lungs expanded to take in the fresh air. The scent of fresh honeysuckle and lavender wafted to her nose and the cooling breeze caressed her face as they ran at a medium pace. Lana talked about her plans for the weekend, informing Taylor she wanted to take her to a fashion show downtown.

Taylor wasn't into fashion or watching waif-thin, beautiful models traipse around half naked, but if her going made her sister happy she'd sit through it. Lana had a real talent for designing fashions herself. In fact, she was constantly doodling in her notepads.

Sometimes Taylor wished that Lana would just leave her, go to college and pursue the career she had been destined for. But as long as these dreams persisted, Taylor knew her sister would never leave her side. The guilt threatened to consume her sometimes. Her sister was young, beautiful and talented and deserved to have an amazing life. She shouldn't have to be a nursemaid to her crazy younger sister.

An hour into their jog the hair on the back of Taylor's neck and arms stood on end. Glancing around curiously, she couldn't pinpoint the source of her unease.

Lana caught her movement. "What's wrong, Taylor?"

"I don't know. I just got this really creepy feeling. Like we were being watched, even followed." Rubbing her hands up and down her arms trying to rid herself of the goose bumps, Taylor shivered in apprehension.

Lana looked behind them, scanning the trees and park benches, but didn't see anything. Some little girls were feeding the ducks down by the pond on their left, a young boy was playing Frisbee with his German shepherd on their right and several other joggers accompanied them on the trail. There were several cars parked at the edges of the park, some were occupied, others were empty, but nothing looked out of the ordinary.

Taylor said jokingly, "I think it's time we got home before I become a paranoid neurotic and have to be put down."

Lana laughed, but kept up her vigil of the park and streets on their way back to the apartment.

They raced upstairs and into their apartment, and Taylor instinctively went to the window to look down below. She saw a car pull up across the street with two guys in it. Frustration, then anger seethed through her. She'd seen that car driving slowly around the park. They had a watchdog!

"That son of a bitch!" Taylor was absolutely seething.

"What? What is it, Taylor?"

Lana joined her next to the window and Taylor pointed at what was, to the best of her knowledge, two undercover cops staking them out. "We're under surveillance. No doubt thanks to our new friend Detective Wills."

Lana chuckled at the sight of the two dark-suited watchdogs drinking coffee. "I told you he was overbearing. Probably thinks we're suspects or something. You know she was our neighbor. How hard would it be for us to go next door and kill her and then make up some bull about you having a vision?" Lana crooked her fingers, imitating putting the last word in quotation marks.

Lana walked past Taylor, grabbed the phone and began to dial.

"Who are you calling?"

"Who do you think I'm calling? I'm going to give Detective Overbearing a piece of my mind."

Taylor flew across the room and jerked the phone out of

Lana's hands, disconnecting the call before it could be completed. "No, Lana. You said yourself that we need to keep our heads about us and cooperate with the police, to give them every piece of information we have."

Lana crossed her arms over her chest and growled, "When did I say such nonsense?"

Taylor almost laughed at Lana's childish behavior. "Last night. And it was some very good advice. If the detective thinks following us will help him solve the crime, then so be it." Besides, although she hated to admit it, knowing the police were close by wouldn't be such a bad idea. "We're innocent, so we have nothing to hide."

Lana gave Taylor a hard glare, as if she were trying to change her mind with a stern look. The phone rang making them jump apart.

Taylor answered in her sweetest voice, "Hello."

"This is Detective Wills. Are you up to answering some questions?"

No matter what she said in her little speech about cooperation to Lana a minute ago, hearing his terse voice brought her anger to the surface once more. "How about are you ready to answer some questions, Detective?"

She heard a thud, like feet dropping hard to the floor. She could almost imagine him lounging back, his feet propped up on his desk, relaxing, while she was doing her best to make it through every day without thinking about the lunatic running wild on the city of Houston.

"I beg your pardon, Ms. Cole?"

"You heard me just fine. Were you planning on informing my sister and me we were to be followed around like we were criminals? Are we suspects?"

He blew out a heavy sigh. "You weren't supposed to know they were there."

"Well, let me tell you something, Detective, if this is the way you guys handle surveillance on people who actually have committed crimes, it's a wonder you ever catch them." She stood next to the window and peered down at their unexpected guests. "I mean really, how many people do you know that sit casually in their cars, in dark suits, dark glasses, drinking coffee and playing cards?"

"Playing cards!"

His shout came through the line so loud she had to pull the phone away from her ear. "That's what I said. I'd say they're playing Go Fish. Honestly, don't you guys have anyone with half a brain on your payroll?"

A muffled sound came through the line before he declared, "I'm sorry. You weren't supposed to know they were there. I just ... I wanted to make sure you and Lana were safe. That's all. You seemed scared last night. Richard agreed you two needed some protection with the killer hitting so close to home." A deep sigh resonated through the line and shivered over her skin raising goose bumps along the way. "As for you and Lana being suspects-- Honestly, the thought did cross my mind. But then I saw your face when you looked at your next-door neighbor's body. You couldn't fake a reaction like that.

"I'm not saying that I believe in all this nonsense, but I have to go with my gut feeling that you are not involved in the killings."

Taylor felt herself brighten at the knowledge that he didn't consider her or Lana killers. She didn't know why, but it seemed like she wouldn't be able to go on if he didn't believe in her. Why her happiness should depend on a complete stranger's acceptance was beyond her.

"Thank you." She bent to look out the window once again and let out a yelp.

"Taylor? What's wrong?"

"Consuela."

Taylor could hear the confusion in his tone as he queried, "Your next-door neighbor? What about her?"

He wasn't going to believe her. Heck, she didn't believe it herself, but there she was. "She's walking up to the apartment building."

"What?"

Taylor hadn't noticed Lana had left the room until she turned searching for her. She needed to know Lana saw her too. "Lana! Come here quick!" As Lana ran into the room all she could do was point out the window. Finally finding her voice, she said, "Please look outside and tell me you see Consuela walking up to the front of the building."

Lana's brows drew together questioningly. Placing a comforting hand on her sister's shoulder, she said in a 'you're not crazy, just tired' tone, "Consuela's dead, honey."

"I know she is, but I just saw her." Taylor looked out the window again, but there was no sign of her neighbor. Turning back to Lana, she blew out a breath, "I saw her, Lana."

"I know you think you saw her, sweetie." Lana looked to the phone and then met Taylor's eyes, "Are you still talking to the detective?"

All Taylor could do was nod. Lana took the phone from her and began talking to Detective Wills.

She had seen her. She wasn't dead; she was down there. Wasn't she? Had it finally happened, had she finally gone crazy?

Was she now seeing ghosts too?

There was a knock at the door. With Lana on the phone, Taylor decided to answer it. When she opened the door, she thought her heart had stopped beating.

There stood her neighbor ... Consuela.

"Lana!"

Taylor heard a loud gasp of surprise followed by the phone clattering to the floor. There was a pregnant pause before Lana bent to retrieve the phone. In the midst of the stunned silence that surrounded her, Taylor heard Lana order the detective to "get here fast."

"I'm sorry, I didn't mean to bother you guys, but there's something I need to talk you about, Taylor."

"But - but you're dead!" Taylor pointed at her neighbor as if to make her aware of whom she was talking about.

"That was my sister, Evita. She came to stay at my apartment for a few days while I was out of town. She ... um, could I come in?"

Taylor watched a few tears slide gracefully down her neighbor's, her *alive* neighbor's cheek. She moved aside to allow Consuela to enter and immediately had the sensation that a huge boulder was being lifted off her shoulders. She wasn't crazy! Yet.

* * * *

By the time Cade arrived, the girls had learned that Evita was Consuela's twin sister. She was staying at her sister's apartment because a man had been stalking her, continuously calling her at all hours of the night, sending roses and love notes to her work and home. The police hadn't been able to stop it, so while Consuela was out of town Evita agreed to stay in her apartment and try to evade the creep.

Consuela patiently went through the whole story again with Detective Wills. Taylor sat by his side and took it all in again, trying to figure out how the Night Stalker would know where to find Evita. How did he know he didn't have

Consuela by mistake?

"Taylor, could you please tell me everything you know about my sister's death?"

Taylor looked at Consuela in shock, then to Cade. "How did you...?"

Consuela waved away her question before it was fully formed. "Mrs. Jones down the hall called me and said that you were seen going into the apartment with the police. I just assumed that all the rumors about you must be true, otherwise why would you be working with the police." She bit her lip. "Did I assume wrong? You're not psychic?"

Taylor didn't know what to do. If she admitted it out loud to someone other than Lana or the police, would it make it more real than it already was? Glancing in Cade's direction she wondered if he would want her disclosing the things she knew.

Cade gave her a hesitant nod, which she interpreted as "give her just enough to satisfy her, nothing more."

How could he read her thoughts like that? Come to think of it, how could she read his?

"Well, since I don't know a whole lot about the stalker problem she was having, I can't say for certain if it was connected. But he knew her name. He called her Evita. Then I thought it was you; I worried he'd killed the wrong girl, but..." She waved her hand in Consuela's direction letting it go unsaid that he had undoubtedly gotten the right girl since *she* sat in front of them now.

"Thank you for being honest with me, Taylor. Was it a quick dea... Did she suffer?" Her voice cracked as the tears began again. She saw that Consuela had loved her sister very much. Empathy filled Taylor's heart. She couldn't even begin to think of life without Lana.

Lana must have been thinking along the same lines

Taylor was because she immediately crossed the room to sit beside her and squeeze her hand tight.

"It was quick. I'm certain she didn't suffer. He's not into torturing his victims, Consuela."

She watched the beautiful girl wipe her tears away and stand. "Thank you for everything. I must be going now. I have some funeral arrangements to make and I still have to inform my parents over in the Philippines of Evita's passing. I just don't know how." There was no mistaking the slight tremble of her shoulders as she drew in a ragged breath. Taylor doubted Consuela was as together as she appeared.

Taylor hugged her neighbor and watched as the girl turned on Detective Wills. "You find this man, Detective. You make him pay for what he did to my sister!"

Cade nodded and said, "You have my word. We'll find this piece of shit and he will be prosecuted to the fullest extent of the law. Pardon my language, ma'am."

Consuela nodded her acknowledgement of his apology and gave him a weak smile that failed to meet her eyes.

Taylor walked Consuela to the door. "If you need anything, don't hesitate to give us a call." They hugged again and Taylor observed Consuela looking at her apartment door covered in crime scene tape, then walk out of the building with her head held high. She was a strong one. She'd make it!

The second Taylor closed the door, Detective Wills was standing a little too close for her comfort. "You have to be careful what you tell people," he said gruffly. "This investigation is extremely important."

"Detective, my sister is doing her best." Lana looked him over from head to toe and threw him a look of impatience before she crossed to stand next to Taylor. "I will not have her harassed in her own home."

"It's okay, Lana. Could you excuse us? I think the detective and I need to have a little chat." Her eyes never left Cade's.

Lana grabbed her arm, forcing Taylor's gaze to leave Cade's and stare into hers. "Are you sure about this?"

She patted Lana's hand and nodded.

"Okay, I'll be down at Margie's if you need me." Lana grabbed her purse off the table by the front door. Before she got completely out the door, she turned and spat out, "If you do anything to upset her, Detective, I will have your job. Do you understand me?"

* * * *

Cade forced himself not to smile at the fool woman's words. Lana thought he was going to hurt her sister. The last thing he wanted to do to Taylor was hurt her. Taylor Cole had been all he could think about since they met.

First, it had been just questions running through his head about the crime he needed Taylor to clear up for him. Cade knew that he'd seen something, recognition maybe, flicker through her eyes right before she fled the room yesterday. She hadn't said, but his cop sense told him she knew what those words in blood meant. But he had a hard time keeping his mind on the case when images of her naked kept intruding.

"Your sister will be fine with me. I just want her to answer some questions, that's all." Cade held his hands up in mock surrender.

Lana seemed to accept that answer, because she blew a kiss at her sister and breezed out the door.

He immediately turned to Taylor, "I'm sorry. I didn't mean to snap at you."

Taylor squinted her eyes, silently asking him if he was

being sincere. She went and sat down on the sofa and patted the cushion next to her. The temperature in the room rose at least ten degrees at the thought of sitting that close to her.

If she kept looking at him like he was the last popsicle on a hot summer day, the temperature wouldn't be the only thing on the rise. God, he had to get his libido under control. He was an officer of the law and they had a serious case to solve.

Getting comfortable on the couch was no easy task with her so close, but he finally settled in. He'd make this short, but sweet, and be gone before his body had time to take in her scent or the way a few stray auburn curls escaped her ponytail and fell across her forehead. She wore big, baggy gray sweats, but the way his groin was aching it was as if she lounged on the couch in some sexy lingerie.

What the heck was wrong with him anyway? This woman wasn't even remotely right for him. She was nothing like his ex-girlfriend or any of the other women he'd dated in the past. She had a flawless complexion, and her hair hung in ringlets from her black ponytail holder. She didn't strike him as one of those women who was high maintenance, but she was definitely a woman who took care of her body.

He decided to get right to the heart of the matter before his mind got out of hand, raking his hand through his hair he blurted, "So we know why you called the victim Evita. But now I want you to tell me why you had such a violent reaction to the words written on the bedroom wall next-door."

"I don't know what those words meant." Taylor looked at him and said slowly and clearly. "I had a *violent* reaction, as you called it, to seeing a girl I knew--well, thought I knew--lying dead not three feet from me."

Cade didn't buy that answer, but he really didn't want to argue with her so he let it go. "I need you to tell me everything you can remember from every vision you've had since the killings started. Anything you saw could help us track this guy down no matter how insignificant you may believe it to be."

Taylor proceeded to tell him everything she remembered. When she left the room briefly to get her notepad, his eyes couldn't help but follow her backside. She looked as good going as she did coming.

He wrote down everything she had in her notebook and hoped some of it would prove useful. Cade noticed her sweatshirt pulling tight across her breasts and decided it was past time to go. After explaining that he would look into her clues and get back with her as soon as he could, he walked to the front door.

Stopping in the hall just outside her apartment he said, "As long as you and Lana feel safe, I'll pull Laurel and Hardy off your tail."

Taylor laughed at his words for the detectives. "Yeah, I think you could give them a break. You know, they may want to go play something other than cards. Maybe Scrabble or Trivial Pursuit."

"I'll suggest them." He chuckled.

"Now, now, Detective. Isn't it all for one and one for all within the police force?"

He sobered. "No, not when it comes to doing your job right. I believe a job worth doing is worth doing well and playing cards while you are supposed to be protecting someone from potential harm is not doing your job well."

"A man with morals *and* dedication. You know, you might not be a big, bad, rude detective after all."

He gave her his best look of utter innocence. "What makes you think I'm rude?"

It was obviously getting harder to control her laughter. "Lana seems to think that you are a little too, um, over the top. She thinks you have the bad cop, bad cop thing going on."

His brows drew together, his eyes alight with mischief. "And what do you think?"

"I think it's time for you to go home now, Detective!" Lana stated loudly from behind Cade.

Taylor hadn't seen her walk up. She hoped her sister hadn't heard her telling Cade what she thought of him.

He lost all the playfulness as soon as he heard Lana behind him.

Taylor hated to see the stern cop return. She had been having fun chatting with the laid-back jokester. "Well, I guess I will talk to you later." She leaned in a little and whispered in his ear in what she hoped was a tone low enough that Lana couldn't hear, "My warden is back."

His eyes crinkled as if he were holding back a laugh. He was so handsome. "I guess it's time to go. Laurel and Hardy will be gone in a few minutes. If you need anything else, call me."

Did he just wink at her?

She watched him as he fled out the door and down the stairs.

"You're pathetic!" Lana burst out.

Taylor closed the door and turned. "What?"

"You're crushing on Detective Overbearing."

"You're crazy!"

"Am I now?"

"I just don't think he's as rude and *overbearing* as you do, that's all." Taylor rolled her eyes at Lana's 'yeah right' face.

* * * *

What was he doing flirting with Taylor Cole? She was a witness--well, sort of. He couldn't get involved with her.

He'd nearly come out of his skin when she leaned over and whispered in his ear, her breath feathering over his neck, rustling his hair. It had taken all his strength not to groan and pull her to him. He briefly envisioned him and Taylor devouring each other right there in front of her sister, showing the bossy know-it-all what they really wanted to do.

He needed to keep his mind on the case. There were women dying out there and here he was thinking about how long it had been since he made love to a woman. Cade had no doubt Taylor's form would mold perfectly to his.

Walking over to the car that held his surveillance team, if you could really call them that, he tried to reign in his temper. His growl almost turned into a chuckle when he saw the cards haphazardly discarded on the floor. These nitwits thought they could make him think they had been doing their jobs.

He dismissed Abbott and Costello, telling them that he thought the ladies would be fine on their own for now. When one of the officers moved his foot, Cade noticed the box for the cards.

Old Maid!

Laughter erupted from him as they drove off. What numbskulls! Ms. Cole would have a field day if she knew what they'd really been playing, although she hadn't been far off.

Shaking his head, he climbed into his truck and set off for home. It was going to be a very long day indeed.

* * * *

Taylor and Lana spent the rest of the day avoiding the subject of dead bodies, detectives or psychic powers. It seemed they had both silently agreed to just be normal for a change.

After making some lunch they settled in to watch their favorite Demi Moore movie. There was just something about a woman who was strong and could kick butt but could also be feminine and ladylike that drew them to the movie. Of course, the Navy Seals master chief in the movie wasn't bad to look at either.

Taylor felt like they were teenagers again, with no worries or concerns to bog them down. She felt free, if only for a little while.

As night drew near, her heart rate accelerated, and she began dreading the time when she would have to close her eyes against reality and meet the harsh darkness of an evil she'd yet to understand. She remembered a time when she hated dreaming about the kids being kidnapped or other crimes being committed. Now she longed for a night where something else happened besides another young woman being murdered.

Since the nightmarish visions started, Taylor tried everything she could to stay awake, but a body could only go so long without rest. That's when she had approached her doctor for some sleeping pills. The first night had been the only dreamless one. Now nothing worked. The dreams even found her when she would try to catch a little shut-eye during the day. They were always with her.

After the movie ended, Lana slipped off to her room under the pretense of reading. Taylor wasn't as naïve as Lana liked to think she was. She'd seen Lana sneak the cell phone off the table and put it in her pocket. Lana had a boyfriend she was hiding from her; she knew it in her gut, but Taylor didn't want to force her sister to tell her before she was ready. When she felt the time was right, Taylor knew Lana would come to her.

She got the sudden urge to call up Detective Wills, but suppressed it fast because that was just not a smart thing to do. Lana already thought she had a crush on the detective. It would most certainly not help matters if she started calling him for no reason other than to just hear his sexy voice. Maybe Lana was right. Maybe she was attracted to Cade.

So what of it!

She was a grown woman. Lana still saw her as a little girl because that's what big sisters do, but it wasn't as if Taylor had never been with a man before. Did it really matter that it had only been one time in her twenty-three years? That didn't make her an innocent, did it?

Shaking off the disturbing thoughts, Taylor decided to try to catch up on her reading. Grabbing the newest book by her favorite author off the shelf, she climbed into her recliner and began to read.

Pulling herself out of the absorbing story, she rubbed her drooping eyes and looked up at the clock. It was past nine o'clock. Where had the time gone? She closed her book and tiptoed down the hall. Stopping at Lana's bedroom door, she peeked in and smiled. Lana was sound asleep snuggled up next to her pillow.

Taylor turned Lana's light off and crossed the hall to her room. Stripping out of the shorts and T-shirt that she put on after showering this afternoon, she slipped on her nightshirt.

Choking down the sleeping pill, she crawled under her blankets. Snuggling down, she dropped off to sleep almost instantly.

* * * *

The stench of rotting meat, hay and horse dung assaulted her. She passed dozens of empty zoo cages. Wrapping her arms around her middle, trying to ward off the cold, she heard her name whisper through the wind. A chill raced down her spine. She knew that voice.

Looking around her, Taylor could see trees in dire need of pruning. A few more empty cages stood off to her left. She read a sign that stood in front of one of the cages. It told of a monkey's breeding and its homeland. Was she in some old abandoned zoo?

Footsteps pounded behind her in time with the beat of her heart. She turned, but saw no one there. Spying a ladder leading to the top of one of the cages, she climbed it hoping to get a look at who or what was calling her name.

When she reached the top, she scanned the ground below her, but still saw nothing. Her heartbeat picked up as she heard her name whispered once again. This time it sounded much closer. She had to get away. She began running down the cage tops, jumping from one to another.

Blood was pounding in her ears. Her heart was beating a steady cadence from the exertion of jumping from cage to cage. The adrenaline burned through her veins.

She noticed something shiny at the end of the trail of cages. Squinting, she tried to focus on it, but it was too far away. She had to get to it. Maybe it would be a clue to help her solve this mystery she found herself starring in.

Some days she even believed that she was still in the coma, just playing a part in her subconscious mind as one of the Scooby Doo gang. Maybe she could be Daphne and be considered beautiful for a change. Detective Wills could be Fred--without the ascot of course.

Her foot plunged through the roof of one of the cages

before she had time to grab anything. A large pile of hay broke her fall. Getting slowly to her feet, she turned at the sound of harsh laughter. A man dressed all in black was on the outside of the cage. He dangled a set of keys by the door, then turned and walked away.

Taylor opened her mouth to yell for him to let her out, but was stopped by the loud growl of an animal standing right beside her. Its hot breath flowed over her face, causing her to cringe. The animal's hunger was palpable as she heard a big tongue flick out to lick its chops. Looking out of the corner of her eye, she saw an extremely large lion stood next to her.

Just as he leaped, she screamed, piercing the still night air.

"Taylor, it's okay." Lana's soft hands were caressing her brow.

Taylor's eyes flew open. She sat up so fast she came mere inches from breaking Lana's nose. "He's at the zoo!"

Chapter Three

Taylor hated calling Cade at three o'clock in the morning, but she had to get the police to search the zoo. She dialed his cell phone number and was utterly confused to find him sounding wide-awake.

Didn't this man ever sleep?

"Detective Wills, this is Taylor Cole. I had a dream our guy is at the zoo."

"The zoo? Are you sure?" She heard a muffled groan and silently wondered if he was wide-awake because he had company of the female persuasion.

She didn't want to think about it. Didn't really want to say anything remotely close to it. But if he was, um, occupied, she didn't want to disturb him. "Detective, am I interrupting something?"

"What?" Another groan followed and she was tempted to just hang up now. The thought of him lying naked with some woman, doing things you only talked about behind closed doors, made her stomach go all queasy. She could almost feel the bile rise in her throat.

"I think I better go. You're obviously ... busy."

"Oh!"

Taylor couldn't tell if that 'Oh!' was because he just received a good feeling or if he finally realized what she was afraid to voice.

"No, Ms. Cole, it isn't anything like that. I'm just icing down my knee. I twisted it earlier when I was playing tennis with Richard."

A blush burned her cheeks as relief washed over her. What an idiot she was for putting her thoughts out there. What would he think of her?

"Ms. Cole, are you still there?"

She heard a sharp intake of breath. Taylor wanted to jump through the phone and soothe his pain. Instead, she settled for, "Are you all right?"

"Yes, I'll be fine." His chuckle calmed her nerves immensely. "I should know better than to play with Richard. He cheats."

"How exactly do you cheat at tennis?" She loved his playful side and wondered if he would be playful in bed as well.

"I'm not exactly sure, but I know if there's a way, he knows it. Now, what's this about our guy being at the zoo?"

The smile slipped from her lips as she related her dream. She wasn't sure if it was a regular dream, or if she had been in someone else's body like before, or if she really had finally gone off her rocker. When she finished her story, she half expected Cade to question her or even appear doubtful, but she was totally unprepared for what he said.

"I'll call the Captain and contact you when I know something."

He believed her. Taylor hung up the phone and held the receiver to her chest, then slowly handed the cordless phone to Lana. There was no doubt in his voice. No skepticism.

"Well, is he going to do something about it, or not?" Lana eyed Taylor, suspicion shining brightly in her eyes. Taylor knew she wore a goofy smile.

"He believed me."

"That's rich. He was probably just trying to get you off

the phone." Lana rolled her eyes at her sister. Shaking her head, she left the room.

"He believed me." It was so amazing it was worth repeating. Her heart swelled with pride and admiration of Detective Wills. He had just given her the best gift in the world ... trust.

* * * *

Cade couldn't believe it. He called his Captain to report what Taylor related to him. They sent officers out to the zoo and had found nothing out of the ordinary. They checked the lion's cages and hadn't found any evidence a woman had been in those cages or eaten alive for that matter.

He didn't want to doubt Taylor's ability or her sanity, but he didn't want to look like a complete fool in front of his fellow officers either. He would go see her later this afternoon and tell her they hadn't found anything, after picking up a few books on psychic abilities. Maybe he could find something to help him understand her better.

When he had realized that she thought he was ... enjoying the comforts of a woman when he groaned on the telephone, he wanted to laugh but thought better of it. He could tell that she was embarrassed. That first groan hadn't been because of his knee though, it had been because he was thinking about her and then there she was calling him. For a moment he thought his dreams were coming true, until she mentioned the Night Stalker.

That's what the papers called the murderer. Cade guessed it didn't matter much to the newspaper reporters that by giving him a catchy name they were sensationalizing him and his deeds. They just liked to give fancy names to criminals so their paper sales would go up. Vultures! That's what they were. Uncaring, unfeeling vultures.

* * * *

Taylor stood in the doorway of the bathroom watching Lana put on her makeup and curl her hair.

Coughing and waving her hand in front of her face to dispel the tons of hairspray her sister just released into the air, Taylor asked, "So, are you going to tell me who you're getting all dolled up for?"

Lana met Taylor's eyes in the vanity mirror. The guilty expression gave her away. "No one. I just thought I would get out for a while." She fluffed her hair, then dabbed on some perfume. "Honest."

"Okay, Lana, if you say so." Taylor was far from convinced, but she was content to wait for her sister to be ready to come to her.

Lana looked like she was about to spill her secret but just clamped her mouth shut and gave a curt nod.

"Just be careful, okay? I don't want to have to be worrying about you too."

"I'll have my cell if you need me for anything. I'm only a phone call away." Lana smiled.

Wasn't she just saying how much she wanted Lana to have a life? *Then why do I suddenly feel so alone?*

Lana wasn't gone an hour before nerves got the best of Taylor. She tried to sit down and read, but the words weren't computing. She read the same page three times without comprehending one word when she finally decided to give it up. She needed a life too. But would that ever be possible with her visions? Any man who wanted her had to accept her abilities and that just seemed to be impossible.

Lunchtime was fast approaching and she wondered if it would be safe to go down to Marge's for a burger and some fries. Since the visions started, she rarely went anywhere alone. An anxiety attack struck one time when she went into the drugstore by herself. She'd thought everyone was looking at her, whispering behind her back. It seemed paranoia struck her the hardest when she was on her own.

Deciding to order a pizza and watch a few movies, she picked up the phone to dial the number. A shiver ran down her spine when she heard a raspy voice call her name. Slowly, she brought the receiver to her ear.

"Hello."

"Taaaylooor."

All the color fled from Taylor's face as her knees buckled underneath her. She tossed the phone into the corner behind the couch as if it burned her to hold onto it. Curling her body into the fetal position on the floor, she began to shake uncontrollably.

"Taaaylooor." It wasn't coming from the phone.

"Leave me alone!" Tears sprang to her eyes.

"I'm coming for you." The whispered voice of her nightly tormentor floated to her.

"Please ... just leave me alone." Taylor's whispered response went unheeded as his words came to her again.

"Soooon, we shall meet."

"No!"

The tears turned into sobs. Sobs of fear. Of pain. They wracked her body and drained her resolve. She was afraid. He frightened her beyond belief.

Taylor had always thought of herself as a strong individual with her feet planted securely on the ground. But this man, this situation, made her doubt herself and her sanity. Was she really hearing him, or was her mind making it all up?

She lay on the floor, completely drained of emotion and tears when she heard a knock at the door. She wanted so badly to run and answer it, hoping against hope she could have her normal life back, but it wasn't meant to be.

"Ms. Cole, are you there?" Cade's husky voice reached her.

She tried to get up, but found her legs still a little weak. Using her hands to crawl up on the couch she called, "Come in!"

Tentatively the door creaked open, revealing the detective holding a large pizza and a six-pack of cola. She could have kissed him right then and there, but all she managed to do was bury her face in the couch cushions and break down in a fit of tears.

Setting the pizza box and drinks down on the kitchen table he crossed to crouch down in front of her. "What is it?" He looked around the apartment, then back to Taylor, "Where's Lana?"

"He ... he was ... was here." Taylor tried to stop her blubbering, but just ended up having hiccups, making a complete fool of herself in front of the one man she wanted most to impress.

Cade was immediately on his feet reaching for his gun. Her hand on his arm stayed his movements.

"No, he wasn't physically here." *I don't think.* "He was calling my name. He--"

Kneeling back down, Cade took Taylor's small hands in his much larger ones. "He what, Taylor?"

Taylor was shocked to hear him call her by her first name. She looked deep into his eyes. Did he think she was a nut job? Seeing nothing but concern, she looked to the corner where she had thrown the phone. "He said he was coming for me and we would meet soon."

Cade followed her gaze to the discarded telephone and then went to the corner and retrieved it. Shaking the phone at her, he said, "Did he call you?"

"No, I ... I picked up the phone to order some pizza and he called my name. I thought it was coming from the phone so I tossed it. But he was still speaking to me after I threw it." She ran her fingers through her hair, dropping her face in her hands. "Am I going crazy?"

Cade had no answer for her. He didn't know what to think of all this. After scanning several books on psychic phenomena, he was still no closer to fully understanding what Taylor was going through. He didn't want to think she might be losing her mind because he was almost certain he was losing his heart to her.

While he went to the kitchen to get some plates, she pulled herself together. He admired her spunk. Maybe that was what attracted him to her, her strength. Most women he knew would have already been locked up in a nice white padded cell.

Taylor was different from the girls he had dated all his life. She had her head on straight even with all she was going through, and she cared about someone other than herself. He'd seen firsthand her love for her sister, her caring for the victims and even for him.

She'd been sincere when she asked if he was all right this morning over the phone. None of his other girlfriends would have given a rat's ass if he were hurt. They would have expected him to suck it up; he was a man after all and pain wasn't supposed to affect them, or so they thought. He could still remember the pain Laura caused him when she left him standing at the altar. But Taylor was different, better somehow.

"Detective?"

"Yes."

Her eyes were questioning as she watched him serve up

some pizza. "Did the police find anything at the zoo?"

He hated to disappoint her. "No, we didn't find anything. No signs of a victim, no signs of our guy. Sorry."

She wrung her hands in front of her and nervously scanned the room. "Oh."

"I don't think you're crazy, Ms. Cole."

Her eyes lit up and he knew he had found the right words to ease her tension. Her shoulders relaxed, her breathing slowed and the most delicious smile played about her mouth. Taking the plate he offered and a drink, she sat on the sofa. He grabbed his plate and sat next to her.

"Thank you for bringing the pizza. But, um, why exactly did you come?"

He watched her pick one of the pepperonis off and suck it into her mouth. The pink tip of her tongue darted out to lick up some pizza sauce that dribbled on her lip. He held back a groan of desire and fought the sudden urge to toss his plate aside, take her in his arms and help clean off the sauce.

"Well, I was on my way here to tell you we hadn't found him and I suddenly got a hankering for pizza. I thought since it was close to lunchtime maybe you and your sister wouldn't mind sharing with me." He looked around the apartment and again asked, "Where is she by the way?"

"She had a date."

Eyebrows raised, he merely said, "Oh." Cade knew Taylor was in the dark about Richard and her sister. He hated not being able to fill her in, but Richard had sworn him to secrecy.

She continued to pull all the pepperoni and cheese off the top of her pizza slices. Once they were all stripped bare, she picked the slices up one by one and began taking bites of the crust.

"Why do you do that?"

Around her hand she garbled out, "Do what?"

"Why do you eat your pizza that way?" He nodded towards her plate.

After swallowing she smiled a big Cheshire cat-sized smile, "My mom used to eat her pizza that way. She said you could taste the pepperoni better if you didn't have to try so hard to chew through the crust part. I guess it just sort of stuck with me."

"She sounds like an interesting lady. I'd like to meet her some day." He smiled back at her.

Tears welled in her eyes and she looked away. "Both my mother and father are dead."

"I'm sorry. I didn't know." His hand moved to cover hers. He meant to just give a comforting squeeze and then release her, but found himself intertwining their fingers. She didn't pull away.

She gave him a watery smile. "You had no way of knowing. It's fine, really."

"If you don't mind my asking, how did they die?"

Taylor shook her head. "I don't mind." She put her plate down on the coffee table, without releasing his hand. He followed suit, allowing her to snuggle up next to him on the couch. "They died in a fire over a year ago. It was an electrical fire. Too many plugs in one outlet or something like that."

"I'm sorry."

"Thank you."

They sat there for several minutes just enjoying the quiet. Her head rested against his shoulder. Cade breathed in the scent of jasmine and lavender. Her scent. He felt his body begin to stir. It felt so right to be holding her so close to him. Sweet, soft skin molded to him, it was so right and yet so wrong. He knew he had to move, to let go, but his body fought him. Finally forcing his arms to release her, his fingers to let her go, he pulled back far enough to read the confusion in her eyes.

"I'm sorry. We shouldn't be doing this."

Her eyes squinted questioningly at him. It was amazing how easily he could read the emotions flowing through her. She gave a quick nod of her head and moved a short distance away from him.

"Would you like me to leave?"

"No!" She held up her hand, and then pulled it back fast. "I ... I don't want to be alone right now."

"Okay. Do you want to watch a movie or something?"

"Yes, that would be great. I mean, I won't hold you here if you need to get back to work." The trepidation he read in her eyes told him all he needed to know. He would stay until Lana returned.

"No, I don't have to be anywhere. It's my day off."

"And I called you this morning." Her hand flew to her mouth. "Oh, my gosh, I'm so sorry."

"It's okay, really." He grabbed her hand and pulled it away from her mouth. "I gave you my card because I wanted you to feel free to call me. Anytime, day or night. Just because they kick me out of the precinct every now and then, doesn't mean I'm not working on this case twenty-four hours a day, seven days a week."

"You're a good man, Detective Wills."

A smile lit up his eyes, "Why, thank you, Ms. Cole. My mom would be proud to hear you say that." He gave a slight bow.

Her laugh filled the room. He loved making her giggle like that.

All through the movie he kept trying to get her to laugh

again and again, even doing his imitation of Tom Hanks' character talking to his true love Jenny. For a time it was like they were just a regular guy and girl sharing some intimate time together with no case or visions between them.

The minute Lana walked in the door the fun, laughing guy disappeared and the all-work-and-no-play cop returned. He made his excuses about following a few leads in the case and bolted from the apartment. As soon as the door shut behind him, Lana started laughing. Taylor gave her best "look what you've gone and done" stare, but Lana just ignored her.

Pointing at Taylor, Lana barely got out between laughs, "I told you, you're crushing on Detective Overbearing!"

"I wish you would stop calling him that." Taylor crossed her arms over her chest. "He's a very nice man." She swept the room with her hand, drawing Lana's attention to the pizza box and three unopened soda cans. "See--he was even nice enough to bring pizza and sodas for us to have lunch."

Lana curbed her laughter and stared at Taylor. "Did something happen while I was gone?"

Taylor didn't want to tell her sister about the voice she heard, but the smile on her sister's lips led Taylor to assume Lana wasn't talking about that kind of stuff. She wanted to know whether Taylor and the detective messed around. *If only.*

Taylor felt the blush creep up her neck. Avoiding Lana's eyes, she said, "I don't know what you mean. We shared a nice lunch, talked about the zoo, where they didn't find anything, and then we watched a movie until you got here."

"Yeah, sure, but what happened that you're not telling me?"

"Lana." Taylor tried to warn her off from questioning her any further, but Lana wasn't having it.

"Taylor." She crossed to stand in front of Taylor and gripped her firmly by the shoulders forcing her to look at her. "I know something happened between you two because you weren't looking at me and you were rambling. It gives you away every time."

"Okay, okay, he held my hand, that's all. Just for a minute. I went a little nuts and he was kind enough to comfort me. Satisfied?"

"No. Not by a long shot, but I'll get it out of you eventually." Lana tossed her hair over her shoulder in that prissy big sister way of hers and went to her room.

Taylor let out a loud sigh. Did she really want to keep secrets from her sister? Well, Lana was keeping one from her, so it was only fair, right? Sooner or later, Taylor would have to tell Lana about hearing voices calling her. She also needed to admit the Night Stalker had seen her in her vision. Cade would have to be told too. Lord, did she dread the day when they found out. She would be in a heap of a mess with both of them for not telling sooner.

* * * *

The breeze was blowing, birds were singing and everything seemed right with the world. The park bench was hard beneath her as she read her romance novel, hoping one day she'd find a wonderful man just like the hero in the book. Caring, loving and honest. Someone who would love her so completely she wouldn't doubt her worth again like she did every day with Tommy.

The sound of the trees swaying in the wind lulled her into another world. A world of peace and tranquility. The alarm on her watch went off and she sighed.

"Time to get back to work. Till tomorrow, my dear." She

placed her bookmark in between the pages and closed it.

Tracing her finger over the handsome face of the man who adorned the cover, she stood and straightened her slacks, brushing any dirt from the bench off the seat of her pants. As she walked out of the park she noticed two people making out on a park bench and groaned. How she ached for that kind of attraction.

Standing on the corner waiting for the Metro bus to come and carry her back to her dead-end job, she thought she would open her book and read a little bit more. She just couldn't get enough. She felt someone bump her, knocking her book into the middle of the street. She made a quick look to see if anyone was coming then stepped off the curb to retrieve her book.

"No!" A familiar voice screamed.

Hands thrust her back onto the curb just in time to feel a whoosh of air from a speeding car. Hearing a loud thud, then the sound of breaking glass, she turned to see Cade being hit by the car. His limp body flew over the hood of the car, coming to rest on the other side.

She'd had this dream so many times since the real accident, it never failed to scare her, but lately it kept changing. Looking down on the detective, she noticed several people were just milling around acting as if they hadn't seen anything. Except one man.

The same man she'd seen bending over her last time was standing on the edge of the crowd that was beginning to form. The Night Stalker was there. Knowing it was a dream, Taylor ran past Cade's body to find the killer.

Spotting her, he took off running down the street. Taylor clawed her way through the crowd of people in time to see him duck down a back alleyway. Racing around the corner, she noticed the walls of the buildings beginning to melt.

Her dream was falling apart at the seams as she followed the man she'd been trying to find for months.

He turned to snicker at her, his scratchy laughter floating all around her. Diving into a doorway, he disappeared. Taylor peered inside the doorway, but it was pitch black. She couldn't see anything, not even the floor. There had to be a floor. He went in, didn't he? She stepped in and immediately plummeted into the black abyss.

As if someone flipped a light switch on in her dream, light illuminated the areas all around her and she realized she was falling fast towards a concrete sidewalk. Her arms flailed wildly, her screams sucked away. The concrete rushed up to meet her. She noticed too late that she was about to be impaled on a metal spike sticking out of the ground.

She awoke with a start right before she hit the ground. Sweat was pouring off her and she felt the fear still running through her veins. Her mind had known it was a dream, yet it still terrified her. Lana came in with a wet washcloth and laid it across her forehead.

"Was it the accident again?" Lana asked as she wiped the sweat from her face.

"Yes, but it was different this time."

She told Lana everything she could remember about the dream. She tried to remember if she had seen any street signs or addresses, but was unable to come up with anything. Lana just took the information and recorded it in the ever-present dream notebook. She never even batted an eye when Taylor told her that Cade had pushed her from in front of the speeding car. The only sign Taylor saw to show Lana even heard her was a little quirk to her lips showing she was repressing a smile.

Lana seemed to think Taylor was falling for Cade. She

felt it could be a definite possibility. But where would that leave them when this case got solved, if it ever did? She didn't know, but she was determined to find out.

Chapter Four

Before the sun even hit the horizon, Taylor was up, going through every one of her books about psychic abilities. She hadn't found one instance recorded where the people in visions were aware of the psychic. It made her feel confident enough to resolve to take control of her life. She made her way to the library to study the books they had. Grabbing several books off the shelf, she found a table in a nice, quiet area and began to read.

She skimmed through more than a few books, but found no instances like hers. Hours later, Taylor stretched and yawned widely after placing the last book on the top of the tall pile. Nothing. Nobody had ever recorded an incident like this.

Grabbing her purse, she stood to leave. The feeling of being watched came over her once again. The hair stood up on the back of her neck and her skin crawled. Oh, she was so going to shoot that man. How dare he put Heckle and Jeckle back on her tail without telling her?

Digging around in her purse, she nearly knocked over the stack of books she'd discarded. Finally her hand wrapped around the small, cold cell phone and dialed Detective Wills. Was it extremely sad that she had put him in her speed dial as number one? Lana had always held that spot, but no longer.

"Detective Wills, Homicide."

"Detective, what is the deal with tethering Tweedle Dee and Tweedle Dum to me again?" Taylor made her way out the front door of the library, feeling angrier and angrier by the minute.

"Ms. Cole? I don't know what you mean. I haven't put you back under surveillance."

Taylor shivered, fear slicing down her spine. If the Bobbsey twins weren't tailing her, why did she feel so dirty? She stopped in mid-stride as she made her way down the sidewalk towards home.

"Ms. Cole, are you there?"

She looked up and down the sidewalk, but as far as she could see no one was around. Scanning the cars for any hint of someone spying on her, she came up empty.

"Taylor!"

"Sorry, I just--well, I just had this really bad feeling. Like before in the park."

"What do you mean before in the park? What feeling?" His sigh resonated through the phone and wormed its way into her heart.

"Like before, when I found your goons following Lana and me. I had a feeling of being watched and then there they were." She started her pace again, chalking her paranoia up to nerves and lack of sleep.

"Are you trying to tell me that you *felt* my officers following you before you saw them?"

She hated to hear the skepticism back in his voice. She had to prove herself to everyone. Why couldn't they just trust her? Who needed to make stuff up anyway? The truth was farfetched enough.

"Yes. The hair on the back of my neck and arms stood up and it was almost like I could feel someone's eyes following me. I'm sure it's happened to dozens of people before. It isn't some cheap parlor trick, like reading tarot cards, Detective."

"I wasn't doubting you." At her audible harrumph, he added, "I wasn't, honest. I just wanted to know how you felt them. I've had those times where I had the sensation someone was watching me too."

"Not the mighty detective." She giggled. "That must have been extremely hard to admit."

"You have no idea."

"Okay, since you didn't sic--" Taylor broke off as she heard footsteps behind her. The panicky feeling returned.

"Ms. Cole, is something wrong?"

It felt as if an elephant had just taken up residence on her chest. She could barely whisper, "I'm being followed."

"Are you sure?" Cade's tension could be felt through the phone.

She slowed her paces then stopped. The footsteps stopped as well. "Yes."

"Get to the police station. Now!"

As she started walking again, briskly this time, the footsteps followed suit. Breaking into a full-fledged run, she sprinted around a small coffee shop and jumped over a bicycle rack. The footsteps followed.

"Help me! Somebody, help me!"

She darted across the deserted two-lane road and ran through an open fence. Pushing past dozens of sheets hanging out on the line to dry, she found herself facing a tall wooden fence with a massive dumpster in front of it. A dead end.

So this was what her life had come down to--dying in some back alleyway while on the phone with the cops. The footsteps following her halted. Squaring her shoulders, she decided she wasn't going down without a fight. Would she be able to make her pursuer stay still until she could dig out her pepper spray?

Sad that here at the end of her life she could laugh at herself. She could almost imagine herself turning towards the would-be attacker and saying, "Pardon me, kind sir, but would you be ever so nice as to wait until I am properly armed before you go murdering me?" The thought of the look of surprise and confusion on her killer's face, wondering if he should kill her or have her committed was almost enough to make her double over in hysterics.

When a hand squeezed her shoulder, she jerked around and swung her purse, hitting a teenage boy square in the face. He fell backwards, sprawled out for the entire world to see. She jumped up and squealed in delight. Then she saw that it wasn't an attacker, and her cheerfulness dissipated. The boy from the library was sprawled on the ground and he was holding her wallet in his hands.

"Oh, my God, I am so sorry. Kenneth, right? I thought-- oh gosh, never mind what I thought--are you okay?" She bent down to help him stand. He was a little shaky but soon had his feet beneath him. "Why didn't you call out to me?"

"You dropped your wallet on the way out of the library, ma'am. I didn't mean to scare you. I have a sore throat so I couldn't call out to you."

Now that he mentioned it she noticed his voice broke several times and sounded extremely scratchy. "I'm sorry. Really."

He rubbed at his jaw. Handing her back her wallet, he said, "What do you carry in that thing, a brick?"

She laughed at his genuine smile. "No, but I think I have the kitchen sink in there. That must have been what you felt."

His scratchy laugh had her smiling, "Well, you might want to check and see if the faucet still works after that hit." He turned and headed out of the yard. She didn't breathe her sigh of relief until he had fully passed through the gate.

"Taylor! Taylor, are you all right?"

Oh, gosh, she had forgotten all about Cade. "Yes, sorry, Detective, false alarm. It was a kid from the library. I must have dropped my wallet when I was trying to get my cell phone out of my purse."

His sigh of relief sounded more profound than hers. Had he been worried for her safety? Did he care about her? Her questions were answered in four little words.

"Come to the station."

Then he was gone. Taylor couldn't believe she'd just acted like a complete idiot. She attacked a kid for goodness' sake. Would life ever be simple again? Oh those were the days ... to walk down the road and not be terrified that some lunatic was about to take your life. Something told Taylor that life would never even resemble normal again.

* * * *

The police station bustled with activity. Officers walked by. Some were shouting at a guy they had handcuffed. Phones rang, doors slammed, and people talked at deafening decibels.

Taylor recognized the officer working behind the front desk. "Hello, Heather."

"Hey, Taylor, how've you been?" The young officer blew wispy bangs out of her eyes. "I was just talking about you the other day with Richard. He said you haven't been feeling well lately."

Taylor figured that Richard and Cade were trying to keep the fact that she was having visions of murder under wraps as much as possible. "Yeah, I've been under the weather."

"Are you here to talk to Richard? Because he's gone to lunch with Lana again."

"Again?" A little light bulb went on in her brain. That little sneak! All this time she had been talking about what a hunk Richard was she had been dating him. Oh, Lana was definitely going to pay for keeping *that* relationship a secret.

Heather's mouth formed a silent O. "Oh gosh, did I let the cat out of the bag?"

The girl looked so innocent and sweet. "No, Heather, I just didn't know that she was eating with him today." Taylor lied and patted the girl's hand trying to dispel any guilt she might be suffering. "Actually, I need to speak to Detective Wills. He's expecting me."

"Detective Wills?" The girl gave her a confused look then gasped, "Oh, he's the hunk in Homicide. Go on in. Homicide is the first door to your left just past the Missing Persons Division." Heather waved her towards the door and buzzed her through.

"The hunk in Homicide, huh?" Taylor giggled to herself. He was definitely that.

As she rounded the corner, she saw the door leading to the Homicide Division. Several desks crowded the room. Men in suits milled around looking rather stressed. When she walked in, all movement seemed to come to an abrupt standstill. The noise died down so fast her head reeled. Everyone was staring right at her.

"Um, excuse me. I'm looking for Detective Wills." When they continued to just stare at her, she began to wonder if batting her eyes and showing a little leg would get a response out of them.

"I'm over here, Ms. Cole."

Taylor followed the sound of the voice. Cade stood in the doorway to a glass-enclosed room. She picked her way across the room, past the many desks strewn with paper.

The men moved out of her way as if she were Moses parting the Red Sea.

"Hi, did you make it here all right?" Cade took her hand and led her into the room.

Taylor looked back over her shoulder and noticed that all the men had turned to watch her. Looking back at Cade she said, "Yes, I'm fine now. Just a little bit of nerves, I guess." She pointed over her shoulder at the men that still stood gaping after her. "Did I do something that I should know about?"

Cade waved her over to a nearby table and closed the door, effectively shutting out the catcalls and whistles that exploded from the men outside. He sat down at the table across from her and quickly swept a folder off the table.

"What was that all about?"

"Oh, that?" He waved his hand dismissively towards the closed door. "They've just been locked in here a little too long is all. They haven't seen the sun or a pretty woman in some time. They tend to get a little rowdy. I apologize for their behavior."

Taylor let that pretty woman comment sink in and take hold of her heart. She had never been called a pretty woman before. Pretty girl, yes, but woman? It touched her that Cade saw her as a woman.

"So what's in the folder?"

"What folder?" Cade tried to look like he didn't have a clue as to what she was talking about. He failed miserably.

Taylor pointed to the spot where he had slipped the folder from the table and now held it underneath. "That folder, Detective."

Cade looked down at the spot where she was pointing and the surprised look he plastered on was absolutely hysterical. "Oh, this old thing. It's nothing, really."

"Well, if it's nothing, why are you acting so weird?" She smiled at him hoping to break through the cop barrier he had erected between them.

"It's just police business, that's all. Nothing for you to worry about." He jumped out of the seat and went to stand next to a small table that held a coffeepot and Styrofoam cups. "Can I get you some coffee?"

Her eyes couldn't help but admire his backside. He looked so good wearing those tight-fitting jeans. His white dress shirt was tucked in and he wore his gun holster over it. His discarded jacket was slung haphazardly over the chair opposite her.

"No, I'm fine, thanks. I should be getting back to the house. Lana probably won't want me to see her here with Richard when they come back from lunch."

"You know about that?"

She had started to rise but stopped dead in her tracks at his words. She turned her head slowly to look at him and felt the anger bubble up inside of her. Everybody knew but her. Lana couldn't even trust her own sister enough to tell her that she was dating Richard, but Cade knew and probably every other officer here.

"I didn't until I got here. My own sister didn't trust me enough to tell me herself! I can't tell you how angry it makes me."

Cade immediately crossed to her and grabbed her arms forcing her to look him in the eye. "Don't get all worked up over this, Taylor. I'm sure once she explains, you'll understand."

Taylor watched emotions flood his beautiful turquoise eyes as they watched her intensely. She forced herself to squirm out of his hold, even though her first instinct had been to curl up into him and hold on for dear life. She couldn't let him affect her like this. She was angry, damn it, and she meant to stay that way.

"If you'll excuse me, Detective, I think it's time for me to go." She headed for the door. She didn't have to stand here and be treated like a child.

"Wait!"

Her steps slowed, but didn't come to a full stop until she had pulled the door open. "I refuse to be treated like I'm some invalid who can't handle the fact that her sister is dating. I knew she was hiding someone, I just had no idea it was Richard."

"They didn't mean to offend you by keeping it from you. I think they wanted to make sure you were going to be okay with them as a couple. If they get married, Lana would be moving out and--"

"Married!"

He grimaced and, holding his hands up in mock surrender, he said, "Okay, I'm an idiot. Could you please just beat the hell out of me and get it over with? Maybe that way Richard will have mercy and not beat me too."

She was furious. They had left her in the dark purposely. But Cade gave her his best hurt puppy dog look, making it hard for her to hold on to her anger.

"Damn you. You couldn't just let me be mad for a few minutes, could you?" She slammed the door closed.

Cade tried his best to hide his smile, but Taylor saw it and punched him in the shoulder as she passed him to sit back down at the table.

Rubbing his shoulder as if she had seriously done damage, he sat down across from her. "Look, I didn't mean to upset you."

Shaking her head she confessed, "You didn't upset me. I just ... I wanted Lana to have a life, but I never knew I would feel so alone when she did. You know what I mean?"

He patted her hand that lay helpless on the table. "I think I do."

* * * *

Taylor waited another hour because Cade wanted to drive her home to make sure she made it there safe and sound. She watched through the glass walls as he met with some of the other officers working in Homicide. He was respected by the other officers, but at the same time appeared to be very laid-back. Just watching his movements, the way he spoke and carried himself, turned her temperature up to boiling.

Climbing in the passenger seat of his truck, she felt the tingling sensation start in the pit of her stomach. The adrenaline surged through her veins, and the sexual awareness kicked up a notch.

When they arrived at her front door, she had the sudden urge to pull him to her and kiss him. She wanted to know what his kiss would be like. But what would he think of her if she jumped him right there in the hallway? Would it be better to ask him in and then jump him? No, better to end with a handshake and call it a day. "Well, thank you for all your help."

He nervously ran his hand through his hair as he jammed the other one in his front pocket. "It was nothing really, Ms. Cole."

"Really, Detective, please call me Taylor." She had heard him say it a few times, but he didn't stick with it. He always reverted back to calling her Ms. Cole. That made her feel as if he had no feelings for her whatsoever. *Maybe he didn't!*

"I'm sorry, Ms., er ... Taylor. I just wanted to try to keep everything professional between us."

Oh, he did, did he? She reached for his hand. Leaning in towards him, she prepared herself to knock him clear out of his bobby socks. The man wanted to keep things on a clearly professional level, did he? She'd show him what for.

"Taylor, I don't think..."

Her lips were a hairsbreadth away from his. "Don't think, Cade, just do."

"What in the Sam Hill do you think you're doing, Detective?" Lana asked aggressively.

Taylor froze. Her lips had parted and were barely touching Cade's. The anger surged up in her hard, making her want to turn to her sister and yank her hair out by the roots. First, she didn't tell her about her love affair with Richard and now she stopped her from having a soul-searing kiss from her own hunky detective. Oooh! Lana was going to pay dearly.

* * * *

Cade didn't know whether to be delighted or angry at Lana's appearance. He could feel the animosity emanating from her.

Taylor's lips barely brushed against his, hinting at what was to come. Her whispered words against his eager mouth reverberated through him as her eyes burned into his, marking his soul. "She is so dead."

He wanted to chuckle. She was so feisty and magnificent. She was even going to kiss him as payback for his little professional speech. He could definitely lose his heart and soul to this woman if he wasn't careful. But he couldn't let that happen.

Clearing his throat loudly, he pulled back from Taylor and shook her hand. "I'll call you tomorrow, Ms. Cole, if anything else comes up."

He was down the stairs and out of the apartment building in a flash. From the looks on the faces of the two sisters, he escaped just in time. Sparks were most certainly going to be flying in their apartment tonight. He could only hope that the police weren't going to be called out.

Reaching his truck, he finally allowed himself to touch his lips where Taylor's briefly brushed.

What would she taste like?

All that temper and strength in one woman. She was intelligent and witty, beautiful and mysterious. She was a dream come true. She was ... off limits.

* * * *

Taylor hated going to bed angry, especially when it was Lana that she was furious with, but it couldn't be helped.

Lana started in on her the minute Cade had left. "I can't believe you were going to make out with that cop!"

Taylor glared. "What about you and Richard?"

She had been furious that Lana and Richard didn't trust her enough to tell her they were dating. They hadn't even bothered to tell her they were engaged. She could handle it. But no! They had to be secretive and treat her like she was some whacko who couldn't be trusted to live alone. The dreams took a lot out of her, yes, but that didn't mean that she had to have a nursemaid twenty-four hours a day.

"That's different. Richard doesn't think I'm guilty of a crime." Lana tried to plead her case.

"Cade doesn't think I'm guilty of anything. And for your information, I am a grown woman who can make out or sleep with anyone I want!" Taylor wanted to tone down the situation. "Look, I know you worry about me getting close to anyone again after the Tommy situation. But I'm a big girl, Lana. I need to be free to make my own mistakes."

"You're right, but that doesn't mean I have to like your decisions." Lana flounced off to her bedroom.

She wanted to run into Lana's room and apologize for being so mean and hateful towards her. She didn't want Lana thinking she wasn't happy that she'd found a wonderful man like Richard to marry. She didn't begrudge Lana a wonderful life. She just wished Lana could say the same thing to her.

Something about Cade seemed right to her. Taylor had never experienced anything remotely like this before. He stayed with her in the back of her mind. She burned with desire and he aroused something deep and primal in her whenever he was near. She had to find out what it was between them because she knew he felt it too. But would Lana ever let her be the grown woman that she was and find out? Probably not. That's okay, she would just have to take matters into her own hands.

She'd apologize to Lana in the morning, then find Cade and see if they couldn't figure out what it was between them that made her burn so hot that she almost exploded into flames.

* * * *

The Night Stalker knew she was awake. Her breathing was almost panting instead of the even breathing of someone sleeping. She didn't want to see him. But he wasn't going anywhere. He was here to take care of business and that was exactly what he was going to do. Slapping her hard across the face brought her eyes open.

The fear was there, shining at him through her pent up tears. He could almost hear the words before she spoke them, "Please don't hurt me. I'll do whatever you want."

Taylor watched helplessly as the young woman begged for her life. The maniac was toying with her, running his knife up and down her body, placing the cold steel of it over her nipples. The woman's body was visibly trembling.

Taylor tried to squeeze her eyes shut against the image as he licked her cheek and raised the knife above her chest. He turned his head in Taylor's direction and whispered, "Are you watching me? I see you." Then he plunged the knife in deep.

Taylor cried out as the young woman whispered, "Help me." Then a piercing scream split the air. She watched as he got off the bed and headed towards the noise.

That was the scream of a baby.

No, not the baby!

But she was powerless to stop him. She was already being pulled from the dream by Lana's voice telling her to wake up.

Tears were rolling down her cheeks as Lana rocked her in her arms. "It's okay, sis. I'm here. You're all right."

"He ... he killed another woman. There was a baby, Lana. A baby!" Taylor had to tell the detective. Maybe he wouldn't kill the baby. Maybe he ... but she knew it was futile to think that the killer had a heart or a soul. He killed all those young women with no remorse whatsoever. He wouldn't think twice about killing an innocent baby.

"Call Detective Wills, Lana."

Lana pulled back enough to look her sister in the eye. "Are you sure? I mean he doesn't even believe you. Maybe I should just call Richard."

"No. This is Detective Wills' case and he needs to know what I know. All of what I know. I will not let this lunatic have any more of my life, Lana. Now call him."

Taylor knew Lana would be outraged for not being told about the killer having seen her, but she would get over it. He knew she was there. There was no longer any doubt in her mind. He had made sure she was there watching before he'd killed that beautiful woman and Cade needed to know that.

Maybe he would be able to help her figure out a way to bait the killer. If the madman could see her, maybe she could get him to make a mistake, to give them some kind of hint as to who he was or how they could find him.

Chapter Five

Too restless to sleep, Cade tried to think about the case, about all those dead women, but his mind kept drifting to the beautiful woman with chocolate brown eyes and unruly curls.

Taylor told him information she had no other way of knowing. But did that make her a true psychic? Richard had used her in several of his Missing Person's cases and was behind her one hundred and ten percent. So was his Captain. So as hard as it was to wrap his mind around it, he had to believe that Taylor was psychic.

Cade had almost kissed her.

He knew he was losing his heart, but if he didn't believe in her ability, could he allow himself to fall in love with her? Was it fair to Taylor, to him? Love and trust went hand in hand as far as he was concerned.

He crossed to the bar in his den and poured himself a neat Scotch. The paperwork spread out across his desk called to him. He was missing something, but what? He sat in his torn leather office chair and stared down at the photos of dead women laid out on slabs at the morgue. What was the connection between these women?

He always had a knack for solving the most difficult puzzles. He possessed a talent for staring at things till the solution presented itself. That was how he'd become one of the youngest police officers to be promoted from beat cop to homicide detective. But something about this case eluded his grasp.

If he could just find it before anyone else got hurt!

His mind swam with possibilities, but he couldn't see how these women were connected. His eyes were heavy and constantly straining to stay open. Cade began nodding off and figured it wouldn't hurt anything if he just laid his head down on his desk and rested his eyes for a few minutes.

The ringing of his telephone jolted him awake. He must have fallen asleep somewhere around midnight. Looking at the clock on the desk, he saw that it was only two in the morning.

Who in their right mind would be calling him at this hour?

He grabbed the receiver ready to tell those dang telemarketers off. "What do you want?!"

"Is that any way to answer the phone, Detective? Not very professional if you ask me."

The fuzziness slowly started to dissipate, letting reality intrude. Lana, the *bossy* Ms. Cole. How in the world did Richard put up with this woman? She must be a tiger in the sack.

Forcing his tone to sound pleasant, "What can I do for you, Ms. Cole?"

He heard a voice in the background whisper something about being nice and then the phone was muffled. "Fine ... I apologize for calling you so early in the morning, Detective Wills, but there has been another attack and my sister wants to tell you about it."

He sat up straighter in his chair, his grip nearly crushing the receiver. "What, another one?!"

"Don't yell at me, Mr. Wills."

God this woman was irritating. He growled his dislike through the phone, hoping that she would get the message loud and clear. "That's Detective Wills, Ms. Cole."

Taylor's voice came on the line, so sweet and demure it made his body vibrate with desire. "I'm sorry, Cade, for my sister's rude behavior. She wasn't the one who got the manners in the family."

He chuckled. She'd actually made him laugh at two in the morning. "That's okay, Ms. Cole. I have a brother that's the same way. Now, she mentioned something about another attack."

"Yes, there's been another murder. I would like to talk to you about it." He heard Lana shout something about pig-headed detectives in her home, then Taylor's soft intake of breath. "I truly am sorry. Could you come over?"

He couldn't quite explain why his body suddenly came to full attention, but if he had to guess he'd say he hadn't been this hard since he was a teenager with his very first hard-on.

Her sultry voice had just asked him to come over. He tried to beat back the excitement that thrilled through him at that moment, finally reining it in before he answered her. "I'll be there as soon as I can."

She sighed and he felt it clear down to his toes. "Okay, see you then. Bye."

Cade held the phone long after he heard her disconnect. *This wasn't a booty call.* He had to get himself under control before he walked into that apartment. He needed to be in full cop mode.

Cade fingered the cold steel of his partner lying on the desk next to him. It had been with him since he came out of the police academy, his backup weapon in case he lost his service revolver or ran out of bullets.

The Kel-Tec P-3AT thirty-eight was small in weight and size, making it unnoticeable underneath his pants leg. It only held six bullets in the clip and one in the chamber, but it was one of his most treasured pieces. It was a thirtieth birthday present from his mother and father.

Slipping it off the desk he headed to his bedroom to get changed. Couldn't very well walk into the Cole sisters' apartment in nothing but his boxers, especially with his body in his current state of arousal. It might undermine his air of authority.

* * * *

Cade sat at the table watching the sisters interact with each other. He couldn't believe his first instinct in this case had been to suspect Taylor of the crimes. When he had gone so far as to think maybe both sisters were involved, Richard had informed him that Lana and him were an item. He had to trust his friend's instincts on this, as well as his own. The girls weren't involved. That left only one explanation for what was transpiring right in front of him.

Taylor knew something more than what she had originally told him, and he wanted to know what that was.

"Look Ms. Cole, you called and asked me over because you needed to tell me something important regarding this case. Can we just get to it, please?" He hated being gruff, especially when he could see the toll this whole thing was taking on Taylor, but he needed to solve this crime. Too many innocent people were dying.

Taylor turned at the sound of his voice. She couldn't help but feel a little turned on by the rough timbre. Did this man even know how gorgeous he was? Shaking the unwanted thoughts from her head she replied, "I asked you to come because I had another vision."

"He never strikes twice within a two week period. Why would he break his *modus operandi* like that?" He raked his hands through his hair, causing Taylor to shiver.

"His what?" Lana glared at him like he was speaking a

foreign language and she was not impressed.

"His MO, Lana. Now stop harassing Detective Wills, okay?" Taylor looked at her sister and gave her best pleading puppy dog look. Lana always fell for stuff like that.

Taylor watched as the sexy detective ran his hands through his hair one more time. Her eyes were immediately drawn to his big, tough hands. Hands that would no doubt feel so good stroking her breasts and then traveling lower to caress her...

What was wrong with her?

She had never been so obsessed with sex before, but this man just oozed male sexuality. Maybe it was his pheromones. *Had he ever had a naughty thought in his entire life?*

"Ms. Cole, are you all right?"

She frowned as she realized that her mind had wandered. Shaking her head, wishing she could take a cold shower to dispel any more unwanted and unwarranted thoughts about Cade, she began to fill him in on the newest victim. She fought back tears as she related the fact that there had been a baby present.

"He's never killed a child before, so I wouldn't worry yourself too much about that." He continued to write down the information about the victim. She hoped he was right about the baby.

* * * *

Cade watched Taylor as she walked into the kitchen and retrieved a glass from the cabinet, then turned his attention to Lana as she took a seat across from him at the kitchen table.

Lana laced her fingers together in front of her and pinned him with those deep brown eyes of hers. He conceded she was attractive. From that perspective, Richard was a lucky man. She was only about five foot six, slim with straight brown hair, cut short to frame her chiseled features. Although he recognized the family resemblance, he was more intrigued by Taylor's brand of beauty. She had an air about her...

Lana asked, "So, Detective, do you still consider us suspects?"

He heard a sharp intake of breath come from the kitchen just as a glass shattered on the linoleum. Both Lana and Cade turned to see Taylor staring blankly off into space, her hands fisted by her side and the glass of freshly poured orange juice pooling on the floor at her feet. Lana reached her first. She shook Taylor, but got no response.

"What's wrong with her? Is she in shock or something?" Cade grasped Taylor's wrist and noticed immediately that her heart rate was skyrocketing.

"She's in a vision! This is how she is at night when she's stuck in a vision. But she's never had one while she's awake."

Cade heard the panic rise in Lana's voice. Something was definitely not right here. He felt it. He was about to ask if he should pick her up and carry her to her room when Taylor's lips began to move. They both fell silent. It wasn't Taylor's voice coming from her mouth.

"You went to the police. That wasn't very smart. I'll find you and take care of you just like the others. Maybe I'll kill you in front of a mirror since you like to watch so much."

The whispered words sent chills down Cade's spine when he realized that this was the murderer's voice, and he had referred to Taylor watching. Taylor had never said anything about him knowing she was there. Had she known?

Turning to Lana he asked, "How do you usually draw her

from these visions?"

Cade's words seemed to finally sink in as Lana snapped back to reality. Grabbing the large dictionary that sat on the kitchen table, she raised it above her head and threw it down hard on the counter next to Taylor.

Blinking furiously, Taylor stared at Cade then looked at the shattered glass shards and orange juice covering the floor. Finally, she turned to Lana. "What happened? Why is he looking at me like that? And what happened to my glass of juice?"

"You don't remember what just happened, Ms. Cole?"

"I ... no, I don't. Why, what happened? Did I black out or something? I haven't had much sleep lately. And would you please call me Taylor and call my sister Lana?" Taylor pointed to her sister and waited for her sister to nod her approval. "I feel a little dizzy. I think I had better sit down."

Before she could take a step, Cade slid one arm under her legs and the other around her back. She fit snugly against his muscular chest, as if she was made to be his other half.

He placed her on the couch and moved a safe distance away from her before his instincts took over and he tried to coddle her.

Lana sat next to her, took her hand and gave it a little squeeze. "Why didn't you tell me he knew you were there? How could you keep something that important from me? I'm your sister, for God's sake."

Taylor didn't know how, but her sister had found out that the killer knew Taylor had been watching. And from the look that crossed Cade's face, he was just putting everything together as well. Great! Now she was going to reap the whirlwind. She laid her head back on the sofa and closed her eyes, took in a deep breath, then let it out slowly.

"Okay, guys. Let me have it."

And they did.

She got it from both sides.

Cade was bashing at her for withholding information pertinent to his case, though she didn't see exactly how it was pertinent to his case. More to her life and sanity. And Lana was enraged at Taylor for not telling her, period. At the time she thought she was protecting Lana from the stalker, now it just seemed irresponsible.

When Taylor was sure they had both talked themselves hoarse, they told her what happened in the kitchen. Fear slithered over her spine and settled in the pit of her stomach.

He found her while she was awake. He sucked her in. *But how?* Why couldn't this psychic bit come with an instruction manual?

Lana excused herself and left the room. Cade took the vacated spot on the couch next to Taylor. She felt his warmth surround her. He started to speak but was cut off by the ringing of his cell phone.

He made his apologies and as she waved them off he answered, "Detective Wills." His breath left him in a whoosh and Taylor jumped. Covering the bottom of his phone with his hand, he turned to face her and whispered, "The baby's okay, he didn't harm him." Then he returned to the phone and responded, "Yes, I'll be there shortly." Worry creased his brow as he glanced at Taylor. "What did it say? Okay, make sure you get good pictures of it. Okay, I'll be there."

Replacing the phone in his hip holster, he reached for Taylor's hand.

"The woman's husband found her when he came home from work. The baby was unharmed. There were words printed over his bed as well as his mother's." He paused.

Meeting her questioning brown eyes he blurted, "Above the baby's bed he wrote 'I see you and you see me, does that make us family?' Above the mother's bed it said..." He raked his free hand through his hair and bolted off the couch, releasing her hand.

"What did it say, Cade?" Her voice shook from the fear she felt at his reluctance to say what had been written, no doubt in blood, above the victim.

"It said 'Taylor.'"

She felt her eyes roll back in her head right before the world went dark.

After a few minutes, she finally came around, only to find herself staring up into the most wonderful deep sea-green eyes she had ever seen. She glanced down at his lips and saw that they were moving, he was talking to her, but she couldn't hear anything over the sound of blood rushing through her ears. Her pulse was racing and the warmth his body was emitting was slowly wrapping around her, comforting her.

Why did she have to feel this way now? Why this man?

"Taylor, can you hear me?" Concern laced his words, concern for her.

Maybe it was possible that he felt something towards her too. If she leaned forward just a smidgen she could touch her lips to his, just a small taste was all she needed. She yearned to find out if he would be gentle and caring, or stern and standoffish. His hand caressed her cheek, and a flutter of sexual attraction sliced through her, pooling deep in her belly.

Never taking her eyes from his lips, she replied, "I'm okay. I just ... I just was a little shocked that's all. I guess I just wanted to believe that it had been my imagination the other day. I really didn't want to know that he knew my name. Now everyone will know."

"So you just thought that if you kept the information to yourself, it wouldn't be real?" Cade brushed his hair through his hair in frustration.

He felt her gaze burn its imprint into his lips. Cade was hit with the almost urgent need to close the distance between their bodies and take her mouth with his, to dip his tongue in and taste her sweetness, to make her forget about all this madness and only feel love and pleasure.

All she'd been through was beginning to show in her eyes, but she wasn't giving in. Never had he met anyone so strong willed. She was determined not to let this sociopath beat her.

"I need to go to the crime scene and retrieve the pictures. Will you guys be okay until I get back?" He looked from Taylor to Lana, making sure he got the thumbs up from both of them.

He hated to leave, but the police officer on the scene said that there had been something weird drawn on the wall next to Taylor's name. Both Lana and Taylor agreed they would be all right, and Cade promised to have a squad car stationed downstairs just in case.

This time as he left, he stopped and glanced back at Taylor and nodded.

* * * *

The drive over to the latest crime scene passed in a blur for Cade. Taylor had somehow managed to wiggle herself under his skin in the three days he'd known her. He had no doubt now that she was having visions of the crimes and the perpetrator. Only now it had gotten complicated because the perp knew her name.

What else did he know about her? The question burned like acid in his stomach at the thought that she might be in danger from this crazed killer.

He met the Crime Scene Investigator, Bart Russo, at the door to the child's bedroom. He ran Cade through all they had, which, like the other crime scenes, was next to nothing. The father had taken the child to a nearby relative's house. Upon inspection of the words written above the crib, a pattern seemed to stand out.

Cade stared at the wall until he thought he would go cross-eyed, but came up with absolutely no ideas about what the image could be. Another pattern was drawn around the writing on the master bedroom wall. He told Russo to get a copy of all the crime scene photos to him by noon. Maybe the symbols would mean something to Taylor.

Leaving the crime scene, he headed for the station. He needed to tell Richard what had happened. He would no doubt be worried about Lana's safety as well. He felt a twinge of jealousy race through him, but pushed the feeling away. Cade didn't begrudge his friend happiness, and if Lana made him happy, then so be it. But he wondered if he would ever be able to find a woman that could make him feel the way Richard so obviously did.

After talking with his Captain and notifying Richard of what had gone on at the apartment, he plopped down at his desk and tried to sort through some of the piles of paperwork piling up on his desk. He'd given all his other cases to the other detectives while he worked on the Night Stalker case. He wasn't working on it alone, but he was in charge, so solving it rested squarely on his shoulders.

The pictures of the crime scene arrived on his desk precisely at noon. Cade spread them out on a table and asked the other officers there to take a look and see if anything jumped out at them. There was a lot of hemming and hawing, but no one had a worthwhile clue. He called to check on Taylor and Lana to make sure nothing further had happened and was surprised Lana hadn't bitten his head off over the phone.

Had Richard interceded on his behalf? If so, he would have to buy Richard dinner. Deciding to call it a day after long hours with no results, he headed home.

Cade fell into bed completely exhausted. He spent all day yesterday thinking about Taylor and the murders, then spent the wee hours of the morning working on the case at the station. She was always in the back of his mind, never far from his thoughts.

Every time he closed his eyes he saw Taylor in a trance standing in her kitchen or fainting at the mention of her name written on a wall.

Now, lying naked in bed, all he could think about was how good it would be if she were lying there next to him. He could almost feel her hands playing with his chest hair, following the trail of hair down his abdomen, past his navel to play with ... oh man, you've got it bad for a woman who either throws up or faints when you're around. He might be sleeping alone for the rest of his life.

He punched his pillow and drifted off to sleep.

* * * *

Although she didn't consider herself an expert on these dreams, far from it in fact, she knew instinctively that this one was different. Never had she seen through the criminal's eyes. The victim's eyes, yes, but never the person committing the crime. Watching as he approached the door that no doubt led to the bedroom of the next unlucky lady, she noticed that he wrote something in deep red lipstick on the door, and then slowly pushed it open.

Blonde, curly hair spread across her pillow, the face of an angel lost in peaceful slumber with no idea she was about to wake up into a nightmare. She shifted in her sleep as he tied her hands to the headboard. Using a pair of pinking shears, he cut through the nightshirt she wore, and then he cut away her panties.

Taylor heard the voices in his head. It was almost as if the little angel and little devil that she saw in cartoons sometimes were visible right there on his shoulders, arguing about whether or not he should do this evil deed.

Concentrating, she heard the voice of reason tell him to stop before it was too late. The killer even seemed to pause, as if he were listening. Then the louder of the two voices screamed out that he had to finish what he started. That they deserved it, they had it coming for what they did to him. The voice sounded evil and malicious, while the other one had sounded almost childlike.

All too soon it was over. He killed her. Taylor tried to talk to him. Maybe he would think she was just another voice in his head. "Who are you? Why do you have to kill?"

She watched as he looked around the room, obviously searching for her. "Where are you? I know you're here." He stopped searching and began to draw on the wall. "Think you can get one over on me, do you, bitch? I'll show you who's smarter."

She felt as if someone had grabbed her by the hair and jerked her out of him. Then the scene faded, and she found herself floating above a bed she didn't recognize. But she most definitely recognized the figure in it. Cade. His bronze sculpted chest was dusted with a sprinkle of brown, curly chest hairs.

Taylor watched as he thrashed around under the covers, dark blue covers littered with pictures of the moon and stars. He mumbled something she couldn't understand.

Silently she wished he would fling the covers off so she could see whether he wore boxers, briefs or nothing at all to sleep in. Suddenly she felt that pull again, pulling her from the room. As the scene faded again, she thought she heard him whisper her name.

Definitely wishful thinking on her part.

Taylor woke to find Lana standing over her. "Hey, what's wrong?" She sat up and pushed her hair back from her face.

"I thought I'd come check on you, since I hadn't heard any screams or anything all night. I didn't expect to find you with a huge smile on your face." Lana smiled. "You almost looked like you were enjoying yourself. Am I to assume he didn't strike again?"

Taylor felt the smile fall fade. "No, he did, and it was really weird, because I was inside him. I heard his thoughts."

Try as she might to focus on the fact that another victim had fallen to the Night Stalker, Taylor couldn't get the sight of a half-naked Cade out of her mind.

Lana's brows drew together as she asked the one question Taylor knew was bound to come, but she didn't know if she should answer it truthfully or not. Did she really want her sister to know of her growing attraction to a man her sister referred to as Detective Overbearing?

"Okay, spill it. What happened that put a smile on my sister's face? I haven't seen you truly smile in so long even if it was in a dream, I thought you'd forgotten how."

Taylor decided to keep her trip to Cade's bedroom a secret for now. "I heard his thoughts. There were different voices arguing about whether he should kill or not. It was weird, that's all."

Something in Lana's eyes told her she wasn't buying that cock and bull story, but luckily she let the subject drop. "I'll go call Detective Overbearing and get the coffee on. Why don't you go and take a nice long bath."

Lana left the room and Taylor fell back on her bed, happy for the fact that in months she had finally slept all night and hadn't woken up screaming and crying. But another woman had lost her life, which caused a serious pain to knife through her heart. Someone had just lost a loved one. She suddenly had the urge to be near Cade. He was so wonderful. He made her feel safe, secure and protected even when he wasn't physically around.

Chapter Six

Cade arrived looking totally wiped out. He had dark circles under his eyes and a grouchy demeanor to go with them. Pulling some pictures from an envelope, he placed them on the table in front of Taylor. They had found the latest victim this afternoon, and the pictures included copies of the photos taken there, as well.

Taylor watched as he went in the kitchen and poured himself a cup of coffee. She was overwhelmed with the feeling that he belonged there, in her apartment, in her kitchen, and maybe even in her heart.

Clearing her throat, she opened her mouth to speak, but found the only words that wanted to come out were the ones she'd asked in her dream. *Did he wear boxers, briefs or nothing at all?* Well, for now, that thought would have to remain unvoiced.

Staring at the pictures, she saw different designs drawn interspersed between the letters. "What do these symbols mean?"

He sat down in the chair next to her, nursing his coffee mug. He blew out a breath as he turned to face her, "I was hoping that maybe you could help us with that."

He took a sip and let out a low hiss. Pursing his lips, he blew gently on the hot brown sludge her sister referred to as coffee.

She was struck by the urge to kiss him. She wanted so badly to soothe the pain the hot coffee had just caused to his tongue. To kiss away his pain and see if there was anything he could do to assuage her own.

She flipped through the photos trying to make sense out of the symbols that winked back at her. "I'm sorry, but I'm not sure they mean anything to me. I don't recognize them."

Cade's shoulders visibly slumped from the weight of her statement. The defeated look on his face made something burst inside Taylor. She wanted to catch this creep for making Cade feel like that, for taking so many lives. Weird that it was no longer about her peace of mind as much as it was about Cade's and the families of those the Night Stalker killed.

Lana entered the dining room looking stunning as always. Her sister was dressed up and grinning from ear to ear. Taylor caught a whiff of her sister's favorite perfume and a twinge of jealousy shot through her. Her sister was so gorgeous. Lana bent and kissed Taylor's cheek, then whispered that she was going to be gone for a while.

"Say hello to Richard for me, okay."

Lana's smile brightened. "Will you be all right by yourself?"

Taylor nodded.

"I'll have the cell with me if you need me. Bye, I love you." At the door she turned and waved at Cade, "Bye Detective Over ... um, Wills." Then she was gone.

"What was she about to call me?" At Cade's questioning look, Taylor couldn't help but erupt into a fit of laughter.

Cade watched Taylor closely as she roared with laughter at the unspoken joke. He couldn't help himself as he joined in, even though he was certain the joke was about him. When their amusement finally subsided, they stared a little longer at the pictures. He described the crime scenes to her and Taylor filled him in on things he left out.

Cade was filled with amazement. Somewhere in the back of his mind he was always waiting for Taylor to pull out a crystal ball and throw out some tarot cards.

When it neared lunchtime, Cade asked, "Would it be unprofessional for me to ask you out to lunch?"

Taylor giggled. "No, of course not." She bit her lip innocently. "Could we maybe go shopping afterwards?" She hesitated as Cade's brows rose, and then rushed on, "I haven't really been out of the house since you brought me back from the police station.

Although Cade truly wanted to squash the shopping idea, he knew she would probably end up going alone, and that wasn't a good idea for her safety or his peace of mind. "Sure."

They ended up choosing Margie's because it was closest. Taylor wanted to walk instead of ride in his truck. He watched in awe as she ordered a burger with the works, a large Dr. Pepper, and a large order of French fries, which she doused in ketchup. He was used to dating women who always ordered a salad and water. A woman who wasn't afraid to eat in front of a man appealed to him immensely.

"You know, Detective, if you don't close your mouth you're liable to catch a few bugs."

She was teasing him. He caught the mischievous gleam in her eye. After apologizing for staring, he dug into his own double cheeseburger.

They passed the time with small talk, both avoiding the one subject that was no doubt foremost in both their minds. It was as if they had secretly decided to take a reprieve and just act like everything was normal.

Taylor so wanted to think of this as a date. She even relaxed enough to talk about her parents' deaths, a subject that she thought had been buried along with them. Cade discussed how he had become a police officer after watching one of his friends get gunned down in a convenience store by another teenager trying to rob it. She heard the tears in his voice.

After they were done eating, they decided to walk the strip and check out the stores there. Three hours later, with her bank account a tad lighter, Taylor was beginning to feel almost human again. Cade had been nothing but nice. He had even given his opinion on some outfits she tried on.

She couldn't help but notice him glancing around every so often. He was a cop and she guessed he just couldn't leave his instincts at the door. Not that she could very well toss her psychic abilities to the side either, but it was nice to pretend. If only for a little while.

Finally deciding she had spent all the money she was allowed to, they stopped for a cup of coffee at the small café a few blocks from home. She stayed out on the sidewalk while he went in since she was loaded down with all her purchases. Cade offered to carry them for her, but she insisted that she was fine.

She watched through the glass as Cade stood in line. He was so stunning. His black jeans molded to every muscle in his legs and his well-defined butt. She wondered what he would do if she walked up and pinched his tush. He wore a black sport coat that she knew was to conceal his gun rather than to protect against the weather, since it was only seventy-one degrees outside.

She knew something wasn't right when the hair stood up on the back of her neck and chills chased each other down her spine. She was being watched again. Turning to scan the sidewalks for anything suspicious, she bumped into a man wearing a hooded gray sweatshirt. Taylor absently uttered an apology, not even really looking at him, and continued to scan the sidewalks. Her mind barely registered his whispered, "Please forgive me."

Taylor immediately clutched at her chest and turned abruptly in the direction the stranger had disappeared in.

"Is something wrong?" Cade handed Taylor her double mocha latte. He followed her gaze up and down the sidewalks then returned to meet her eyes as her brows rose in astonishment.

Her latte fell from her hands and spilled on the sidewalk. Cade moved just in time to avoid the hot liquid. Her hand flew to her mouth as she blurted, "He was just here, Cade! He bumped me!"

Confusion crossed Cade's face then as the meaning of her words hit him full force, he grabbed her hand and said, "Which way did he go? What was he wearing?"

"He was wearing a gray hooded sweatshirt and blue jeans. I didn't see his face, but he whispered 'Please forgive me.' That's how I knew it was him! It just didn't dawn on me until you came out."

"Which way, Taylor?"

She jerked her thumb in the direction the man had fled. Cade pulled his gun from his shoulder holster and told her to go inside and call for backup. As he ran off in pursuit of the man who had haunted her life for so long, she whispered, "Be careful."

* * * *

Cade's heart was pounding. His brow broke out in a sweat. He ran down the sidewalk checking every alleyway, but he saw no sign of anyone wearing the clothes Taylor had described. She could have imagined it or it could have been just an average Joe walking down the street that bumped her. But his cop's sixth sense told him that neither one of those scenarios were correct--it had been their guy.

He knew her name, he could easily find out more about her if he wanted to. The guy was good. Cade had to be better and for Taylor's sake he prayed that he was.

Thirty minutes later Cade returned to find Taylor standing inside the coffee shop, staring out the window. Her face had the words 'terrified beyond belief' written all over it. They'd been so close. That demented son of a bitch had gotten close enough to touch her. A chill ran up his spine at the thought of what could have happened to her. His thoughts were reflected in Taylor's eyes.

How could he have been so stupid as to leave her out there on that damn sidewalk?

He could have lost her. He tried to think about what his life was like before he met her and found it hard to bring any memories to mind that didn't include her smile, her warmth, or even her brow creased with worry.

Cade longed to hear the sound of her laughter again. The yearning to know what noises she would make while he was buried deep inside her made his whole body ache. But his job was to keep her safe, not fantasize about taking her to bed.

Taylor called Lana and related what happened. Lana promised to meet them at the apartment. They rode back to her apartment in the police cruiser that came for backup. Taylor didn't seem shocked to find Richard at the apartment with Lana.

Cade immediately pulled Richard into the kitchen to give him a full rundown. After they returned to the living room, Richard walked over to Lana and kissed her on the cheek, whispering something unintelligible in Lana's ear. She giggled.

Cade said, "Make sure you lock the door behind me. The surveillance car is parked downstairs if you should need anything." He was a few steps from the door when Taylor's hand on his arm stopped him cold.

He turned to face her, his features unreadable. Before Taylor could think about her actions she was kissing him. His lips were so soft, warm and willing. When his arms circled her, she melted against him and he dipped his tongue in to taste her. Somewhere in the back of her mind, she heard a soft gasp of surprise escape Lana, then the muffled sounds of retreating feet.

When she finally ordered her arms and lips to release him, they were both breathless and aching. She felt a blush burn a path from her cheeks to the tips of her ears, then she bubbled out, "Thank you for everything today, Cade. I did have a good time, considering everything."

He was left speechless. She'd kissed him as a thank you. He merely muttered, "You're welcome," and left. Cursing the whole way to the car, he knew he would most definitely not get any sleep tonight. He'd felt her warmth, tasted her sweetness and she had fit so perfectly against him that he ached. She was perfect for him in every way and she'd kissed him as a thank you.

* * * *

Taylor took two sleeping pills. After the day she'd had, she really needed sleep. Slipping into her red silk oversized nightshirt, she caught her reflection in the mirror hanging over her dresser. "Oh, honey." She pulled her hair back away from her face and then turned from side to side. "No wonder he looked at you funny when you kissed him. My lord, you look like something the cat hacked up."

Grabbing the pad and pen that was always on the nightstand by her bed, she feverishly wrote down things to do tomorrow.

Facial.

Haircut.
Pedicure.
Manicure.

If she was going to attract the hunky detective of her dreams, she was definitely going to have to do some major construction work.

Chuckling to herself, she realized how literally Cade had been the man of her dreams just last night. She still remembered those sheets. Who would have guessed that a grown man would have sheets with moons and stars on them?

Climbing into bed, she silently prayed for a peaceful, dream-free sleep. Well, she wouldn't mind too terribly much if her dreams included Detective Overly Cute.

* * * *

Blinking furiously and rubbing her eyes, Taylor tried to wake up. The alarm clock told her it was eight o'clock. The sun shone through her blinds, slicing her comforter with rays of sunlight. Taylor sat up and stared at the dust motes highlighted by the sun's rays. She had slept all night and couldn't remember having any dreams.

The pills had finally worked! She must not have been taking the right dosage before.

Taylor was so wrapped up in her happiness that the ringing of the phone caused her to jump. Smiling she reached for the phone on the nightstand, hoping to hear the sexy voice of the man in her life. "Hello."

The voice that greeted her was not one she wanted to hear now or for the rest of her life if she could help it.

"Good morning, Taylor," the raspy voice whispered. "Did you enjoy your dreamless sleep last night?"

"How did you ... how did you know about that? How did you get this number?" Panic flowed through her body as she felt the bile rise in her throat.

She heard a scratchy laugh. "I know more about you than you think. Have you seen your sister this morning?"

A gasp escaped her. *Lana! Not Lana!* She held the cordless phone pressed hard to her ear and slowly walked towards her bedroom door.

"Are you there yet?" His whisper grated down her spine, causing goose bumps to rise on her arms and legs. Something definitely wasn't right. Her sister was always up early. Of course, that was usually because she had to wake Taylor from a vision. *Please God, not Lana!*

She opened her door and looked across the hallway to see that Lana's door was shut. Lana never shut her door. Crossing the hallway, she slowly turned the knob and inched the door open. She heard his laugh on the other end of the line, but ignored it as she pushed the door open a little more. It was too dark to see. Lana had black blinds and thick black curtains to keep out the morning sunlight.

Reaching her hand in, Taylor flipped the switch and immediately dropped the phone. Lana lay on her bed, her hands tied to the headboard, a gag in her mouth and her clothes cut off. A single red rose lay across her belly.

Taylor ran to the bathroom and threw up.

Minutes passed before the retching subsided, but the tears continued to flow. The bastard had been in her home. He took away the one family member she had left. A thought struck her that terrified her even more.

He could still be in the apartment.

Using the bathroom counter to support herself, she moved to the door and peered down the hall. Both her bedroom door and Lana's were still open. The phone lay forgotten on the floor. Looking down the hall towards the living room Taylor listened for any movement, but couldn't make out anything. Coming out of the bathroom, she kept her back to the wall. Slowly she tiptoed down the hall. She had to get to Lana's cell phone on the kitchen counter and call Cade.

Stopping at the corner to look around for any sign of the intruder, she whispered, "Where are you?" Switching walls, making sure she stayed firmly pressed to the wall, she continued to make her way towards the kitchen. Just as she reached the front door, a loud knock sounded, causing her to jump away from it and shriek.

"Taylor, is that you?"

"Cade!" Her tears fell as she realized how glad she was to hear his voice. Unlocking the door, she fell into his arms.

Cade took in Taylor's disheveled appearance and tear-streaked face, and then glanced at Richard. Holding her body close to his he felt her trembling. "What is it? What's wrong?"

Taylor was sobbing uncontrollably. The one word he could make out was "Lana." Richard was down the hall in the blink of an eye. A loud audible cry and a few choice curse words were heard before Richard yelled for Cade to check the apartment.

He brought Taylor back inside the apartment and gently removed her hands from around his waist. Drawing his gun, he told her to stay right behind him. She merely nodded, but her sobs quieted down. He went from room to room, turning on lights and checking every cabinet and closet. When they were done checking the rest of the apartment, they entered Lana's bedroom.

Cade heard Taylor's deep intake of breath and felt her grab a handful of the back of his shirt. He looked over his shoulder at her, knowing that his confusion was written clearly upon his face. When he turned to look inside Lana's room, he realized why Taylor had been so panic-stricken.

Lana's body was covered with a sheet from the bed and Richard was untying her hands from the headboard. Taylor laid her head down on his shoulder. He felt her trembling. Her tears were silently soaking his shirt. When he saw Lana's chest rise and fall, he released a breath he hadn't known he'd been holding.

"She's alive, Taylor, look!" He pointed towards the bed.

Taylor raised her head, unwillingly, but needing to see if Cade was right. *Could Lana really be okay?* When she saw her sister's eyes open she knew her sister was all right. Richard rocked Lana back and forth, whispering words of love. She pushed past Cade and rushed to the bed. Plopping herself down hard on the edge, nearly pushing Richard off, she pulled Lana from Richard's arms and hugged her tight.

Trying to swallow the lump of emotion that rose in her throat. "Are you all right?"

"He must have drugged her. She wasn't hurt, just tied up." Tears fell from Richard's eyes.

Her eyes were drawn to the phone still lying on the floor where she had dropped it earlier. Cade followed her movement as she crossed the room to pick up the telephone. She raised it to her ear. "Are you still there, you freak?"

Cade and Richard both stared at her. They both looked completely confused.

"Yessss!"

Cade ripped the phone from her hands and yelled into it. "Stay away from her, you hear me, you psychopath? I'll catch you!"

Taylor's face was one of shock as she watched Cade. Gone was the cool demeanor, and in its place was a fierceness she had never seen before. She heard the laugh and then the click as the shadow that terrorized her life hung up. Cade pressed the off button and threw the phone across the room with a loud curse.

Eyes closed, Cade leaned his head back against the wall, trying to close off the anger that threatened to consume him.

He should have been here. This was the second time in as many days that he had almost lost her to this crazy whacko. Resolved to finding this sick bastard, he knew there was only one way to keep Taylor and Lana safe till that happened. He pushed himself away from the wall and began barking orders.

"Richard, take Lana to the hospital and make sure she really is okay. Then take her somewhere safe." He turned at Taylor's sharp inhalation. Pointing a finger at her, he stated in his best no nonsense voice, "And you, go pack some things, you're coming with me."

Cade knew instinctively she was going to argue, he braced himself for it. So he was completely taken aback when she nodded and said, "Okay." Then in a flash she was gone. He shook off his confusion at her compliance.

While Richard busied himself packing, Cade sat and talked to Lana to try to keep her awake, letting her know everything would be okay. She was still very groggy from the drugs.

He was going to solve this and they could get back to their lives. He could only hope that he would do it before this son of a bitch got to Taylor.

* * * *

Taylor hugged Lana and they said their good-byes in the parking lot. After wiping away her tears, she climbed in the passenger seat of Cade's truck. During the entire drive to his house, Taylor didn't speak one word. Staring out the window, watching the traffic pass in a blur, seemed to put her in a trance.

Cade pulled into his driveway and shut the engine off. "Are you okay?"

When she turned away from the window he saw the fat tears rolling down her cheeks. "She could have died and it would've been all my fault!"

The sobs she'd been trying to hide from him left her in a whoosh. He pulled her onto his lap and wrapped his arms around her, allowing her to cry it out. "It wasn't your fault. None of this is your fault, Taylor."

"But why me? Why do I have to be the one with this curse?" She wrapped her arms around his neck, laying her forehead in the crook of his neck.

She smelled so good, felt so right. He knew he could lose himself in her arms. Cade pushed a strand of hair behind her ear. "I don't know why you, but maybe you should stop seeing this as a curse and see if we can't figure out a way to make it work *for* us."

Her sobs had quieted down, the silence punctuated by a few hiccups as she tried to compose herself. Cade was sure she would strike out at him once she realized where she was sitting. He wasn't prepared for her sweet mouth to be kissing and nibbling its way up his neck.

A lightning bolt zinged through him as she reached his lobe. Her teeth closed around it tugging hard, then licking, sucking till he groaned his approval.

His hands wouldn't behave themselves and follow his strict orders of "hands off." Sliding up her knee to her waist, then slipping under the hem of her T-shirt, he heard her quick intake of breath. Her head fell back on a moan as he grasped her breast, thumbing the nipple, pinching it to a hardened response.

Twisting, trying to get closer to him, her elbow hit the horn, jerking them both to a complete stop. Taylor's eyes were filled with wonderment and a little bit of remorse.

Taylor crawled back to her side of the truck, straightening her clothes the best she could in the close quarters. They both muttered meaningless apologies for getting carried away. She grabbed her bag from the backseat and leaped out of the truck.

Chapter Seven

Cade got out of the truck, slamming the door a little harder than necessary, and walked her to his front door. His house wasn't bad for a cop's salary. It was in a nice neighborhood, the lawns were all mowed and some were littered with kids' bikes or toys. He didn't appear to have a problem living around kids.

Upon entering the house Taylor thought she had died and gone to heaven. Finally a man that could clean up after himself. The place was spotless. No dirty laundry lying on the floor. No dirty dishes piling up in the sink, growing mold or some other type of science experiment. His shelves even appeared to be dust free.

Cade must have read the surprise on her face because he laughed and then stated dryly, "I have a maid. She comes twice a week."

Taylor couldn't hold back her laugh. "I should have guessed. No man is this neat." She made a stabbing motion with her finger towards the living room, foyer and kitchen area.

"Whatever do you mean? Men, not neat? I'm shocked and appalled at that remark." He placed a hand on his chest trying to feign shock, but failed miserably.

"Stop it!" She swatted at his hand.

Sobering, he looked deep into her eyes and told her, "I'm usually pretty neat. You know, I do my own laundry and stuff, but when I'm working on a case my head seems to become entrenched in it and I can't find time to clean up after myself."

"Well, that's understandable. Just tell me that it's not your mother coming over to clean up after you, and I promise not to laugh at you again."

"Liar."

Crossing her finger over her heart she blurted, "I cross my heart and hope to die." Stopping herself at the reality of how close she had come to just that, she decided to rephrase it. "I mean ... I promise." Taylor saw Cade's body flinch at her words.

"It isn't my mother. And you don't need to worry about anything, okay? He won't find you. I promise." Now it was his turn to cross his heart.

As he gave her the complete tour of his home, he explained to her that he had other bedrooms but didn't have any extra beds. She thought for a moment that he was going to suggest they share his bed. He blew her away with his offer to sleep on the couch.

When they entered his bedroom, she stared at the comforter covering his bed. It was red flannel patterned with big bright yellow smiley faces. She smiled.

"I liked your moon and stars sheets better."

Cade wrinkled his brows in confusion. "How do you know what kind of sheets I have?"

Taylor opened her mouth to speak, knowing full well that it was too late to withdraw the foot that she had so strategically placed inside. He wasn't supposed to know that she had visited his bedroom in one of her dreams.

Cade held up his hand before she could tell him. "I don't really want to know how you knew about my moon and stars sheets, do I?"

Taylor shook her head.

"Well, then let's leave it alone. For now."

Taylor meekly replied, "Okay."

"Are you hungry? I could order us a pizza or something."

Cade ran his hand through his hair, suddenly nervous standing in his bedroom with the one woman he had wanted there since they'd met. All his energy was spent trying to keep from reaching for her and touching her the way he had in his truck. He longed to feel her respond to him again.

"Pizza sounds fine. Make mine with pepperoni, Canadian bacon and jalapenos."

"Ah, a woman after my own heart." Cade clamped his mouth shut, silently cursing himself for being such a fool. Then he noticed that she was trying her best to keep the blush that was creeping up her neck from spilling onto her cheeks.

She failed.

Cade started to back out of the room. "I'll just go order the pizza. Make yourself at home."

* * * *

By the time the pizza arrived, Taylor was famished. Cade had elaborated on some of his ideas to decorate and fix up his house. He enlightened her about his two older brothers and his baby sister and all of their kids. He even let it slip that he wanted to one day have a family and hear the laughter of children bouncing off of every wall.

It wasn't often that Taylor found a man who admitted that he wanted kids. She found she was developing a great respect and admiration for the man she saw before her. He was sexy and intriguing, but down to earth and very easy to talk to.

They cozied up together on the couch and munched on pizza and drank soda till they thought they would pop. They whiled the day away watching movies and talking.

When it got late and Taylor knew she would have to go to bed soon, Cade seemed to read her mind and see her unwillingness to allow herself to sleep. He reached into a small drawer in the side of the coffee table and brought out a deck of cards.

"Want to play a little poker?" Cade waved them under her nose as if issuing a challenge.

"What, you want to play with me? Aren't you afraid that I can read minds and will beat the pants off you?" Taylor giggled with delight as she watched his brows raise in question. She had him actually wondering whether she could or not.

Finally, he released a long, slow breath and ran his free hand through his hair. He whispered, "God, I sure hope you can't."

That got another bout of laughter from her. If he knew how much she wished she could read his mind she would be in deep trouble. If only she knew what he wanted from her. She wanted him, there was no mistaking that, and from what had happened in the truck, she surmised that he was attracted to her too. But was a romp in the bed all he wanted? Could he possibly be interested in more than a one-night stand?

After clearing the coffee table off, they took their respective sides. Taylor watched Cade shuffle the cards. If he played half as well as he shuffled, she was in big trouble. He did the bridge without one single card flying loose, then he fanned the cards out on the table, and then magically made them all stand up and fan out again.

She was in *big* trouble!

"So, what'll it be, my dear?" He raised and lowered his eyebrows in an attempt at some lecherous, evil look.

She giggled, then sobered immediately at the look of

pure, unadulterated lust in his eyes. "Well, strip poker is definitely out of the question." She laughed at his crestfallen face. "How about we play five card stud?"

Reaching around behind her, she grabbed one of the decorative pillows off of the couch and placed it behind her back. Leaning against the pillow, she snuggled back into it, making sure she was comfortable. Cade's eyes followed her every move.

"Are we going to just play or are we betting?"

It seemed as if Cade was in a trance. He stared straight at her as if he hadn't heard her speak. Then abruptly, he shook his head, grabbed the bridge of his nose between his thumb and index finger and pinched.

"Are you okay?" Taylor reached across the table and grabbed his wrist, tugging on his arm trying to dislodge it from his nose.

Looking up at her, his eyes alight with mischief, he said, "Yeah, I'm okay. I just had a vision."

Taylor's hand dropped immediately. *Was this stuff catching?* Her hand flew to her chest. "What?"

"I had a vision." He paused so long Taylor wondered if he was going to tell her what it was he saw. "I saw you ... in my kitchen ... cooking."

Taylor was going to strangle him that's all there was to it. He was going to rue the day he ever made fun of her. "Oh, did you now. Because I could have sworn that I had a vision of you waiting on me hand and foot. Oh, and speaking of feet, you were giving me a darn good foot rub."

His smile was almost her undoing.

"Well, I guess we've figured out what we're betting. Let's get down to business." Cade doled out the cards like a professional dealer from some casino.

She was definitely in trouble!

Taylor was right. In the middle of their fifth game, she knew she was a goner. He was taking her to the cleaners, but good. Taylor threw her cards at him, hitting him right in the chest.

"Now, don't be like that, darling. I can't help it if I'm the master at playing cards. I let you win one, didn't I?"

Taylor wanted to smack that smug grin right off of his face. Instead of that though, she decided she could get back at him easy enough. A smile split her face. "I guess you win, Detective Cheater. But what exactly was it that you won again?"

"You know very well that you just earned the right to cook me a homemade meal right there," Cade pointed towards his kitchen, "in my dream kitchen."

"Oh, right." She dragged the last word out. "I guess before we made that bet, I should have told you that I can't cook, huh?"

Cade's jaw dropped. She strained to keep a straight face. He was so adorable. Taylor watched his jaw open and close, trying to form a coherent response. As he swallowed, she followed the movement of his Adam's apple.

"You can't cook?" The thought seemed to be foreign to him. Obviously he hadn't met a woman who couldn't cook. Well, he still hadn't, but he didn't need to know that at this moment. Besides, his distress was well earned.

Taylor shook her head and mouthed the single word, "Nope." Her insides hurt from trying to keep her laughter at bay. He was going to be surprised in the morning. She jumped up and towered over him. He followed her movements. With his mouth still agape, she whispered, "Good night, Cade." She bent down and kissed him on the cheek and bounced off in the direction of his bedroom.

* * * *

It was an enormous feat trying to get comfortable in Cade's bed, knowing that he lay just a few feet down the hall, but somehow Taylor managed. The minute she slipped into the dream, she was aware that it was going to be a strange night.

Thick clouds of steam came at her from all directions. Tunnels led off in different directions to places unknown. When she heard the whispers start, Taylor immediately thought she must be in the killer's head again. Preparing herself to try to talk some sense into the man, to make him turn himself in to the police, she stopped moving. A figure lying lifeless on the floor stared up at her.

The man was slightly obese, probably weighing in around three hundred pounds or so. Since his body was crumpled in a heap, she could only guess that his height was somewhere around five feet four to five foot six. He had brown, shaggy hair and a small silver stud earring in his right ear.

From the looks of the marks around his neck, she would have to guess that he had been strangled. Taylor figured she must be having visions about a different murder because the Night Stalker only killed women. He didn't kill men. That, plus the fact that this man was obviously strangled had her relaxing the muscles that had involuntarily tensed up at the thought of seeing the Night Stalker commit another crime against a defenseless woman. But it didn't quite explain the whispers.

Stepping past the body, she tried to determine where she was so she could notify the police where to look for the murder victim. Following the sounds of the whispers down a tunnel to her right, she nearly jumped out of her skin as a huge rat ran past her. It was long and plump with an extremely long tail. When it squeaked up at her, goose bumps broke out all over her arms. The sensation felt like a thousand spiders all began crawling on her at once. Nasty little rodent!

Insane, that's all there was to it. She'd gone insane, jumping like a little girl at the sight of a rat, but not even batting an eye at a dead body.

When she came to a fork in the tunnel, Taylor headed off towards the left since some light could be seen coming from that direction. Several feet down the corridor a wooden door stood in her way. Light could be seen through the cracks in the wood and from underneath. She moved through the door effortlessly.

Looking around, she gaped at what lay before her. A stained and moldy mattress lay on one side of the room. A gray, moth-eaten blanket was haphazardly thrown across it. A large, scarred wooden table dominated the room. It was littered with newspaper clippings and several different types of Bowie knifes. The one man she was hoping not to see tonight occupied a worn wooden stool.

He wasn't wearing his mask, but his face was turned away from her. All she could see was his broad back, hunched over a pile of newspaper clippings. His whispered words floated to her.

"All for me. So beautiful."

Taylor didn't want him to know she was there. Silently, she willed him to turn around so she could see his face. When he reached up to place a picture up on the wall above the table she strained to catch a glimpse of his face.

Instead her eyes were immediately drawn to the picture he had just placed on his 'wall of terror.' That was the only suitable name for it. The wall was plastered with pictures of women, alive and beautiful. Some of the women's pictures had been colored on with red paint. At least she hoped it *was red paint. Bile rose up in her throat as she stared long and hard at her picture. It was just a headshot. Her hair was blown back off of her face and a smile was visible. It was soon joined by a full body shot.*

"Oh, my gosh!"

The picture took her back to the day she'd bumped into him on the streets. There she was standing in front of the coffee shop holding her bags full of goodies. She was looking towards the coffee shop, no doubt admiring Cade's backside. It had been him. She hadn't imagined it. And now he had a picture of her hanging on his wall.

She felt violated. She felt sick.

"I'm coming for you, Taylor. Soon we will meet."

Taylor sat up in bed dripping with sweat. Her breathing was ragged and her heart hammered loudly in her chest. She frantically looked around for Lana. Gulping down air, she slowly realized that she was in Cade's bed. Lana wasn't there, but she was still safe.

She lay back down and quietly sobbed into her pillow. She wanted this nightmare to end.

* * * *

Cade lifted his head and attempted to rub the crick out of his neck. He'd fallen asleep on his desk again. If he didn't stop this maniac soon, he was going to find himself in desperate need of a good chiropractor. Looking around, he tried to determine what it was that had awakened him. Finally deciding he hadn't missed an important phone call, he laid his head back down. Instantly his head sprang back up, sniffing tentatively and then more deeply.

Pancakes. Bacon. Eggs.

That damn woman lied to him. She could cook ... and magnificently if the taste measured up to the smell. Slipping into his jeans, he padded barefoot to the kitchen.

Taylor was bustling around his kitchen like a pro. What a liar she was. He smiled as he watched her go about her business oblivious to the fact that she was being watched. She flipped an omelet out of the pan, up into the air and then caught it with all the pizzazz and style of any highly paid chef. She slipped it out of the pan and onto the plate without even touching it with a spatula.

He applauded.

Taylor set the pan down on the top of the stove and turned the burners off. Grabbing each side of the apron, she curtsied. "Thank you, kind sir." Straightening, she met his eyes with a little trepidation. "Your breakfast is served."

When her eyes immediately looked away from him, Cade looked down and blushed. He'd put on his jeans and zipped them, but hadn't bothered to button them. And in his haste to follow the tantalizing scents wafting to him, he neglected to put on a shirt.

"Sorry. I'll be right back." Trotting off in the direction of his bedroom, he hoped to find something suitable to wear. Something that would cover up his morning erection which only got stiffer as he watched Taylor flit around his kitchen. She seemed to fit, almost like she was meant to be there.

He slipped on a comfortable pair of sweat pants and a big, baggy T-shirt. Maybe the baggy clothes would help to hide his interest in the beautiful cook in his kitchen. Returning to the kitchen, he noticed the table was set for two and his mouth was watering. But was it from the aromas coming from the plates or for the delectable woman before him?

The cook looked so enticing in her cut-off jean shorts, showing off what must be miles upon miles of shiny, beautiful legs. Her T-shirt with a yellow smiley face reminded him of the first day they'd met. Her 'Have a nice day!' shirt had the same smiling face on it.

"Well, let's dig in before it gets cold." Cade moved around the table to hold Taylor's chair for her.

Her whispered "thank you" was almost unintelligible.

"I thought you said you couldn't cook?" He sat in the seat across from her. Cade was tempted to pull his chair around so they could sit side by side, but something about the way she was holding herself aloof this morning made him think twice about it.

Taylor looked through her lashes at him shyly. "I had to get back at you for your smugness about winning, didn't I?"

Cade chuckled. "Yeah, I guess I was kind of a jerk, wasn't I?"

She held her thumb and index finger up, indicating the size of an inch. "Just a wee bit. But you were cute doing it." Her hand dropped and swooped up the fork to dig in.

So she thought he was cute, huh? He could work with that.

"I am pretty cute, aren't I?" His chest puffed up and he grinned.

"Just eat your food." Stabbing her fork in his direction, she tried to cover up her smile with her other hand.

Cade raved about her food from the minute the first morsel touched his lips. "We definitely need to play cards more often."

"Oh, really." Taylor watched as he smiled that devastatingly handsome smile.

"Yeah, that way you will be forced to cook all my meals." He ducked as she threw a piece of bread at him. They both laughed, but he could tell something was still bothering her.

When they finished eating, Cade surprised her by getting up and washing the dishes. She tried to help, but he waved her away saying, "You cooked, I'll wash." Just as he

NIGHT STALKER   109

finished up the last bit of silverware, the phone rang, startling Taylor. Cade figured she must be remembering the last time she had answered the phone and it had been the Night Stalker. There was no way he could imagine what she felt when she thought Lana was dead. Grabbing up the phone he spoke briefly to the caller then hung up.

Taylor nearly jumped clear out of her skin when she felt a hand grasp her shoulder and squeeze.

"Sorry." Cade released her. "I didn't mean to scare you. That was the station. I need to go in for a few hours. Will you be okay?"

Mentally trying to calm her nerves and slow her heart rate back to normal, she whispered. "Yes, I'll be fine."

"Are you sure? 'Cause I could have someone come sit here with you." Cade started to punch in numbers into the receiver.

Taylor grabbed his hand and took the phone from him. "I'll be fine, really. Go do what you need to do. I brought some stuff to keep me busy."

"I..."

"Go!" She pointed towards the front door and pretty much ordered him to get out of his own house.

Glancing towards the door then back at Taylor, he said, "I'll be back as soon as I can." He bolted for the door, grabbing his wallet and keys off the small rectangular table by the door. It wasn't until he was already gone that Taylor realized she hadn't told him about her dream and the dead man.

* * * *

Taylor hated to admit it, but she missed Cade. She knew it was irrational when he hadn't even been gone but a few hours, but there it was. Loneliness.

After trying several times to sit down and read one of the

many romance novels she'd hastily packed in her duffle bag, she gave up. Every time she read about a stolen glance or a kiss that was sure to melt the paint right off the walls, she thought of Cade. Then she started to miss him even more.

Taylor cleaned up as much as possible. She made the bed and put her dirty clothes in the washer. But Cade's maid had done a very good job in keeping his home nice and neat, so she had nothing to do. Nothing to do, but wait. And wait and wait and wait.

Eventually she gave up trying to concentrate on yet another talk show about transvestites in love. She decided to explore the house to see if she could learn more about Cade, something that she didn't know already, maybe even something he wouldn't voluntarily disclose to her.

The books lining the shelves in his office were definitely eye-catching and very telling. There were tons of criminal justice books. Books on crime scene investigations, forensics, even a few on race car driving and gardening. But what surprised her most was when she came across the books on supernatural abilities. Several caught her attention because of the yellow post-it notes marking pages he had highlighted and even written in notes and questions.

He was reading up on her powers of clairvoyance.

Was it because he wanted to know more about her powers? Because he cared about her?

Or was it because he was afraid of what she might be capable of doing?

She hoped it was because he cared. Either way, she felt weird reading the questions that he had written, as though she were invading his privacy. It wasn't like she was reading his personal journal, but she just felt wrong somehow. Replacing the book on the shelf, she left his office and decided to lie down on his bed and breathe in his scent until he got home.

* * * *

Taylor felt the scream build up in her lungs. She was caught in someone's embrace. They held her so tight she couldn't move.

Had he found her? Was she in another dream?

She opened her mouth, ready to let loose the loudest scream she could muster, considering that her lungs could hardly draw a breath.

"Don't scream, it's just me."

The whispered voice sent hot molten lava straight to her nether lips. The chills she felt tickling the hair on her arms wasn't from horror or disgust but from excitement and pure heated lust. Cade held her tight against him. His warm breath feathered across her neck. A small smile tilted the corners of her lips.

"You were having a bad dream when I came home. You cried out and I couldn't get you to wake up, so I tried this instead. It seemed to calm you down."

She snuggled back against him, firmly cementing his groin to her rear end. She felt his arousal against her backside, and he drew in a quick breath. "Did I hurt you?" She grinned.

"You know very well what you just did, so don't play Miss Innocent with me."

He sounded mad, but she couldn't make her smile fade no matter what she tried. He felt good pressed against her. Being held in his arms felt better than anything she could ever remember. Giggling, she wiggled her butt closer to the throbbing heat that was quickly solidifying behind her.

"Whatever do you mean, Detective? I'm not aware that I did anything to you." She added one final wiggle.

His hand grasped her hip in an attempt to still her movements. "Taylor, if you continue to do that, you're going to embarrass both of us."

Now she was completely confused. "What do you mean?" She turned her head to look into his eyes.

He laughed. "Let's just say I've only come in my pants once in my life. I was a teenager, a virgin, and a voluptuous lady brushed by me in a store, grazing my groin and whoops, there I went. So unless you are prepared to help me clean up my mess, I suggest you quit moving that delectable bum of yours against me like that."

His meaning fully dawned on her, and she moved her body away from his. She quickly turned her head away from him when she noticed he was staring at her. "I'm sorry."

"No, you're not, you little vixen."

Taylor whipped her head around so fast she damn near broke his nose. "Who are you calling a vixen?" she asked with a hint of sarcasm tinting her words.

"You! Admit it. You were curious what I felt like. I bet you're thinking about me naked right now, aren't you?"

"You, sir, have an ego that is a little too big."

He ground his groin into her backside causing her to jump. She might have come off the bed had he not been holding her so tight. "My ego isn't the only thing that's big, baby." He laughed at her horrified gasp.

She tried to wriggle out of his grasp. He made a strangled sound and then moaned while Taylor continued to try to wrench herself free from him. "Ooh, oh, oh, Taylor!"

His grip loosened and she crawled out from his arms. With her feet firmly planted on the floor on the opposite side of the bed from Cade, she stared down at him. His eyes were glazed over and halfway closed. A small tilt to his lips gave her an immediate explanation to what all the moaning and groaning was all about.

"Did you just... You didn't just do what I think you did, did you?"

Cade's grin stretched across his face and his hand pointed to the evident wet spot on the front of his pants. "I told you not to move like that. Didn't I?"

Her eyes grew wide with the acknowledgement.

Quirking a single eyebrow upwards, Cade said, "And it's your job to clean up the mess you made."

Taylor's knees buckled out from underneath her and she broke into laughter.

Cade crawled to the edge of the bed to observe her getting a good laugh at his expense. It was impossible to hold a grudge against her for giving him his first orgasm since Laura--without the use of his own hands at any rate--so he decided to join in.

When their laughter finally came to an end, he said, "I'm going to take a shower and change my clothes." He could see she was holding in another laugh as he stood up from the bed. The wet spot was still visible, but so was the fact that he was still fully aroused. God, what he wouldn't have given to have been inside her when he exploded.

To have her come with him.

Who was he kidding? He was falling for her and no amount of professionalism was going to keep him from having her.

Next time! If there was a next time, she would come first. He guaranteed it.

Chapter Eight

Cade cursed his traitorous body the whole time he was standing under the ice-cold spray of the showerhead. He'd come all over himself because Taylor had wiggled her bottom a little too close. *Oh, God, what she must think!*

She was probably having a good laugh and pledging never to sleep with a man with a premature ejaculation problem.

He couldn't remember a time in his life when he'd had a problem satisfying a woman. Never allow yourself to climax before they do. That was his policy. But a few little jiggles from an exquisite woman and he was like Old Faithful, erupting every few minutes. It was amazing he was able to walk upright in her presence considering the constant state of arousal that he was in.

The thought of taking her to bed and embarrassing himself further by not being able to perform at his best sent a shudder through him. What if he couldn't satisfy her? What if she laughed at him and he couldn't get it up?

Why had he allowed that back-stabbing wench, Laura, to steal his confidence from him?

When she'd left him, she didn't just pack up and say, "Sorry, I don't love you anymore." No, she had chortled and said, "Sorry, Cade, but I found someone who is capable of satisfying me in bed. Oh, by the way, all those so-called orgasms you gave me, well I faked every last one of them." She'd moved out without even so much as a backwards glance for old time's sake. He hadn't been able to bring himself to make love to another woman since.

He'd tried several times while out drinking with the boys to be interested in a few women that had blatantly flaunted themselves at him. Had even gotten one woman to his home and to the couch, half-naked, before deciding that it wasn't such a good idea. Cade never thought of himself as the kind of guy who could just have casual sex. He always made it a point to know his partner, even to care about her, before having sex.

He wasn't a complete idiot.

Realizing he'd come to care very deeply for Taylor in a short amount of time was painful as much as it was enlightening. Satisfying her was the only thing on his mind. If he couldn't make her happy and keep her sated, Cade didn't know if he would be able to live with that knowledge of failure. Taylor was special in so many ways.

Toweling himself off, he decided on some jogging shorts and an old blue police academy T-shirt. Headed into the living room with an apology for embarrassing her on the tip of his tongue, he stopped dead in his tracks. He was speechless.

Taylor stood in the middle of his living room, bent over at the waist, her delectable rear end in the air. Blue spandex pants clung to every curve. A scrap of material that resembled a bra encased her abundant breasts. She started to bounce lightly, stretching the muscles in her legs.

Cade was in a trance. His eyes followed every bounce, every sway of her breasts, of her hips. He eased himself down on the couch, watching every movement as she continued with her stretching. His jaw dropped open and nearly collided with the floor when Taylor stood up and grabbed her right foot, bringing it up parallel with her head. She was doing a perfect split while standing on one foot.

Her flexibility amazed him. Inwardly, his male hormones were screaming for a chance to see what he could do with all that in a bed. The positions they could accomplish, the pleasure...

When she released her leg and went back into the original stretch a groan escaped him. He watched as her eyes flew open and peered at him through her split legs. Her face was beet red, but he seriously doubted it was from the blood rushing to her head.

Damn! He'd embarrassed her again.

"I'm sorry. I couldn't ... I was ... impressed by what you were doing."

Straightening, she turned to glare at him. "You were groaning." A smile lit her eyes. "Do you have another mess you need to go clean up by any chance?"

"You're harsh." He gave her his best wounded, sad puppy dog eyes. "I still think I deserve a little 'kiss it and make it better' session. You've wounded my male pride, woman."

Giggling, Taylor sat down next to him and patted his knee. "And here I thought I helped to relieve a little built up pressure."

Cade growled at her.

"Ah, come on, Detective. Can't stand a little harmless fun?" Her hand slowly crept up his thigh towards the 'injured pride' in question.

Cade grabbed her hand before it got too close to its target. "Watch it, Taylor. You don't want to bite off more than you're willing to chew."

"Would you do a favor for me, Cade?"

His grip tightened slightly, then slowly released her hand. "Name it."

"Would you teach me a few self-defense moves?"

His mind reeled. Here he'd thought she was about to ask

if he would ravish her. Take her to heights she'd never seen before. Hell, he'd even had the fleeting thought that she wanted him to take her to see Lana, but he hadn't been prepared for her to request this.

"Why?"

"Well..." She rose from the couch and began to pace in front of him. It took every ounce of his strength to keep his mind on her question, instead of watching her graceful muscles bunch and relax as she paced back and forth. "I want to be prepared in case the Night Stalker finds me. I'm a fast learner and I..."

"He won't find you here." Cade had to stop her. He wouldn't allow her to start him thinking about all the possibilities of danger that could come to her.

Taylor's eyes burned into him as she stared long and hard. "You can't guarantee that, Cade. He found out my name. He found me on the streets while we were shopping. He has my picture up on his damn wall. He..."

Cade was off the couch and across the room in the blink of an eye. "How do you know he has a picture of you on his wall?"

Taylor looked away from him quickly. "I had another vision. I saw where he's living. He has a wall full of pictures of smiling, happy women. He put my picture up on the wall." She wrenched herself from his grasp and took his abandoned spot on the couch. "He had pictures of me from that day. I didn't see his face, but he told me we would soon meet face to face."

Her trembling was visible from his spot across the room. She was shaken badly by this guy. Cade ran a hand through his hair and tried to muster up some courage, courage to face what was fast becoming a nightmare. The thought of that crazy man touching Taylor, hurting her, was too much for him to bear. If teaching her some self-defense tactics would help keep her safe, then he was more than willing to teach her.

"Later I want you to sit down with me and describe everything from that dream, okay? But for now I'll teach you anything you want me to. Whatever makes you feel safe."

An hour later they were still going strong. Taylor hadn't been kidding when she said she was a fast learner. He knew guys on the force who hadn't grasped the basics of self-defense in as little time as she had. He'd taught several ways to break out from different types of holds that perpetrators would try, even showing her the surefire way to get out of a full nelson.

Of course, wrestling around with Taylor on the floor was wreaking havoc with his hormones. Several times she'd caught him off guard as his mind slipped to other things they could be doing that were more enjoyable than self-defense moves, other things that would cause her breathing to become shallow and force little hesitant pants from her. Other moves that would cause her to sweat. Just the touch of her silky skin beneath his fingertips was enough to almost drive him over the edge again.

He felt his legs being swept out from underneath him again, as his rear made hard contact with the carpeted floor. Thank goodness he had gone with thick padding under his carpet. Thank goodness he'd gone with carpet, period. With as many times as she'd taken him down to the mat, so to speak, he would have needed to see a doctor by now. As it was, he probably had some pretty nice sized bruises on his derriere.

But it was all worth it for the chance to have her straddling his torso like she was right this very moment.

"You lose. Again." Her hands grabbed his and lightly pinned them above his head.

They both knew that he could overpower her if he wanted too, but it made her feel better to be in control so he allowed her to think that she could take him. Oh, God, how he would love it if she would take him.

Take him inside her. Take him in her hands. Take him in her mouth.

This line of thinking was only going to lead to disaster if he didn't learn to control his libido.

Pretending to struggle against her hold, he squirmed and twisted underneath her. But it only served to intensify his longing. He felt her heated center rubbing back and forth against his abs. If he didn't miss his guess, from the feel of moisture as well as a musky scent that could only be coming from her state of arousal, he wasn't the only one affected by their little bout of foreplay.

That was the proper term for what they were doing. The training session had ended long ago, and now it was merely two bodies rubbing and clinging to each other in a vain attempt at looking like they were teaching and learning self-defense tactics.

"I could never lose with you on top of me." He hadn't meant to say that out loud, but there it was just the same.

Her eyes darkened and her body trembled slightly. "I'm flattered, Detective. But wouldn't it be a winning situation if I were perhaps here," she slid lower until her feminine heat caressed his already aching erection through their clothes, "instead of on your stomach?"

"Woman, you're killing me." He couldn't hold back the growl that rose from deep down.

"I know. Isn't it wonderful?"

Her giggle was short-lived as he flipped their positions

and ground his stiffened rod against her moist heat. The look of surprise on her face was almost his undoing. "Is it wonderful now, you wanton woman?"

A smile split her face as she began to rock her hips up and down and side to side. "Most definitely."

He gripped her hips to stop her motion before he embarrassed himself once again. "Taylor, stop it! You're going to cause another accident if you don't stop."

"I'll behave." At his comical expression of disbelief she added, "I promise." Crossing her fingers over her heart. "Scout's honor."

"I very seriously doubt you were ever a scout or that you'll behave."

"Cade, how dare you think me to be a woman who doesn't uphold her word. I'm shocked." She turned her head up as if she was a snobby, rich lady that had just been insulted by the help.

Releasing her hips, he placed his hands on either side of her head. "I'm sorry, I shouldn't have doubted you."

Her head snapped to attention as her hips again began to bring him to the brink of ecstasy. "How sorry are you, Cade?"

"Not so sorry that I won't take you over my knee, young lady."

"Promises, promises."

He brought his mouth down on hers, hard. Her lips met his and opened for his sweet invasion. Their tongues dueled and fought for control, sipping each other's sweet nectar and sharing the taste. She tasted like cinnamon and strawberries. Her lips were as soft as a rose petal and just as silky. Thank the lord she had stopped gyrating those delectable hips against his raging erection.

Pulling back from the sweetest, most erotic kiss he'd ever

known, he stared down at her. Her breasts rose and fell as her breathing became erratic. The brush of her hardened peaks scraping against his chest was enough to push him over the edge and force him to take her right there on the floor in his living room.

"I want you so bad, Cade." Her breathy murmur forced his gaze to find hers. Looking away from her bountiful breasts was sheer torture until he stared into her eyes and saw the want and need he was experiencing reflected in her chocolate brown eyes.

He rested his forehead against hers and whispered back, "I want you too. So bad I hurt, but I don't think it would be a good idea for us right now."

Her warm breath caressed his cheek, as she moved to place a chaste kiss against his lips. "I'm willing to wait."

Four little words that in other circumstances would be merely words held the power to form a lump the size of the Golden Gate Bridge in his throat and make his heart cry out. He was falling so hard for this woman, a woman that he was pretty sure he had no future with. He rolled off her and stared up at the ceiling.

"So, Detective, what is on the agenda for today?"

And just like that, her mood was changed from hot and erotic to all work.

"I wanted to look at those pictures again and see if maybe looking at them with fresh eyes would help us locate him before he kills again." He blew out a heady breath and regarded her out of the corner of his eyes. "Maybe that dream you had will jog a memory when you look at the pictures."

He saw weariness mixed with a sense of determination flash through her eyes. She was a tough woman, all right. She sat up and squared her shoulders, ready to take on the world. His little powerhouse. *His?* When had he started thinking along those lines? He shoved the question to the back of his mind and mentally stamped it for future scrutiny.

* * * *

Six hours later, they still had no clue what the pictures meant. Taylor just saw a bunch of squiggly lines. Nothing that really resembled much of anything. Cade was extremely patient and understanding in the hours since their little encounter. No man had ever inspired her to be so wanton, to be slick and ready for him to take her at the mere brush of his hand against her skin. Cade awakened so many things inside her that she'd never known existed.

Taylor had been prepared to let him take her right there on the floor like she was some sex-deprived hussy, but he'd put on the brakes. It took every last shred of dignity she had not to allow his dismissal to injure her heart. He'd wanted her, that much she was sure of. She didn't know exactly why he didn't take what she so blatantly offered to him, knowing full well most men would've been hard-pressed to turn down an offer so direct and to the point.

Cade tossed pictures across the table, bringing her mind back to the present. This case was taking a toll on him as much as it was on her. His hair was mussed from the dozens of times she'd witnessed him running his hands through it.

Standing, she pushed her chair back under the table and started to grab all the photos and place them into a neat pile. Glancing down at the pictures as she grabbed them up, she tried one last time to figure out what the drawings in each might mean, stopping at the one that displayed her name written in some poor woman's blood. Ice water ran through her veins at the thought of how close Lana had come to losing her life to this guy.

Why did he kill all these women? What had they ever done to deserve to lose their lives?

What had she done to deserve this power of sight?

"Are you okay?" Cade's warm fingers clasped her wrist. She looked at him and dropped the picture that she held in her hand. Without warning, Cade's face grew worried and fear seemed to grip him.

She opened her mouth to ask what had put that look on his face, but no words came out. Her eyes rolled back in her head. A vein beat a steady tempo at her temples as the world went black around her.

* * * *

Taylor saw a small convenience store across the road. As she walked closer to get a better look, she saw two young boys jokingly pushing each other around out front. They both looked around thirteen or fourteen years old at best. Brown hair worn a little too long, with big baggy clothes that made their gaunt figures appear even smaller than they were.

They slapped each other on the back and then slipped inside the store. One of those boys had looked so familiar, yet she couldn't quite place a name to his face. She secretly hoped she was not about to witness another child abduction. It weighed heavily on her heart if the police weren't able to get there in time to save them.

She hurried across the street and peeked through the glass front doors of the small mom-and-pop store. She saw the boys grab some bottles out of the barrel that held ice and cokes. They seemed so happy and carefree. Suddenly, as if someone turned on the light switch, it hit her as she stared long and hard at the two boys how she knew one of them. There in front of her stood a much younger, more relaxed Cade. The young boy next to Cade could have passed for his brother, they looked so similar in height and stature.

She watched helplessly as a man at the counter turned towards them and flashed a gun their way. Cade froze, but the young boy next to him didn't. He apparently hadn't seen the gun. Cade's hand flew out to try to stop his friend from moving any further and in the process dropped the coke he was holding. The roar of a gun firing followed the sound of the glass bottle breaking against the floor.

The young boy flew backwards, landing a few feet from Cade. Cade immediately dropped down next to his friend and began sobbing. Cradling his friend's head in his lap, he yelled out the only word his young heart could possibly think to ask, "Why?!"

His eyes flew to the man holding the gun, only for Taylor to notice that it wasn't a man after all, but a boy no older than the one he had just shot. "Why'd you kill my brother?" Cade's sobs twisted her heart, but his words shredded it in two.

She'd been right. There was a family resemblance. Cade had told her about this day, the day that made him want to become a police officer, but he never mentioned that it was his brother that had been killed. He'd said it was a friend.

Taylor watched in horror as the young boy holding the gun raised it to his temple and pulled the trigger. Cade's voice broke on a sob as he yelled out, "No!"

Two young men had lost their lives that day and one had been forever changed.

* * * *

"Taylor! Taylor, talk to me. Please!" Short of slapping her awake he'd done everything he could think of. He'd tried splashing her face with water, tried dropping a large book on the table, afraid that she'd been pulled back into a vision again. Nothing seemed to bring her out of it.

Reaching for the phone, determined to contact Lana and see what she suggested, he heard a whimper escape from Taylor's lips. He rushed to her side and saw that her eyes were open and she was alert. He dropped down on his knees next to the couch where he had placed her when she fainted. He caressed her forehead.

"Are you okay? What happened? I was so worried. I thought I'd lost you, and then you wouldn't wake up and I tried everything and..."

"Whoa, slow down. I'm still seeing spots here. One question at a time, okay?" She tried to sit up. He helped her to a sitting position, then sat next to her, pulling her into his embrace.

"You had me so worried." He nuzzled her neck then placed a soft kiss on her temple. He rested his chin on top of her head, taking in her sweet scent.

"Why didn't you tell me it was your brother?"

Her words came out in a hushed tone. He had to strain to hear her. "What? What was my brother?"

She pulled back from his embrace and turned to face him. "Your brother was the one that got shot that day in the store, not your friend. Why didn't you tell me it was your brother? Why lie?"

He wasn't sure how, but she knew the truth about the day that had changed his life. How could he tell her that the death of his twin brother had taken a part of him? How did he explain to her that it had been *his* best friend holding up the store? Two people he loved beyond reason had been taken from him that day.

"I... How did you know that?" He tried to stand, needing to stretch his legs and run from the memory he wanted to forget.

She grabbed his hand forcing him to stay sitting, forcing him to look into her eyes, filled with compassion and--was that love? "When you grabbed me, I must have received some form of energy from you. I was thrown into your thoughts I guess, because I saw that day as if I had been there in the flesh. I saw you and your brother joking outside the store. I saw you grab cokes. I watched as that boy," she swallowed through the lump in her throat, "shot your brother and then took his own life."

The silence stretched out for what seemed like hours. Finally he sighed deeply. The time had come for him to face his past. And oddly, he wanted to talk to Taylor about it, to make her understand why he was so driven when he was working a case.

"He was my twin brother, Kendall. The boy holding up the store was my best friend, Randy." Taylor's gasp was almost his undoing. He felt the tears welling up in his eyes. Blinking furiously to try to make them disappear, he hurried on. "We had all gone there to hang out. You know, boys' night out.

"Back then there wasn't much to do on Friday nights, so we hung out at the gas station. Randy went in to use the restroom and when we got tired of waiting for him, we went in and decided to get some cokes."

Cade ran his hand through his hair. "I don't think Randy intended to shoot anyone, especially Kendall or me, but when I dropped the coke because I was shocked to see Randy holding up the place, he must have jerked when the glass shattered. The bullet caught Kendall right in the head. He died instantly."

Taylor's hand squeezed his. He hadn't even realized she'd still been holding it.

"I didn't even get to tell him that I loved him and he was gone. I saw Randy's intention when he brought the gun up to his head, but the words to stop him came too late."

He reached up and felt the wetness dampening his cheeks. He couldn't remember the last time he'd cried. It hurt to think that he hadn't even cried at his brother's funeral. He was glad that the tears finally came to mourn his brother's and his best friend's deaths. None of it would have happened if not for Taylor and her magical presence in his life. He had her to thank for so many things and the list just seemed to grow with each passing minute.

When Taylor's delicate fingers brushed the tears from his cheeks, the urge to pull her against him and ravish her mouth was strong, to taste her sweetness and wrap himself in her warmth.

Chapter Nine

Cade settled for pressing his lips to the palm of Taylor's hand. Her sweet sigh scorched his skin. It felt like his skin had been set ablaze. Blood rushed through his veins. The sound could be heard pounding in his ears with every beat of his heart.

Cade couldn't believe the way that Taylor made him feel. He'd felt lust before, but never so strong. She really seemed to care about him and all that he'd gone through. When he looked into her eyes, he didn't see sympathy for the death of his brother and best friend. He saw understanding, caring for the young boy who watched two people he loved die needlessly, love for the man that he'd become because of that fateful day.

So, could he say without a doubt that what he felt for Taylor was lust, plain and simple? The answer was a simple, soft-spoken, "No." Was it love? Could he possibly have fallen completely and hopelessly in love with Taylor Cole? That answer was simple too. Yes.

But knowing his feelings didn't tell him how she felt about him. She hadn't said anything that would lead him to believe she loved him, but then they hadn't really known each other that long either.

While he was busy analyzing his feelings for Taylor, she had slipped down to her knees between his legs. Her hands were steadily creeping up his thighs. The look in her eyes was nothing but pure desire. She'd said she was willing to wait, but.... With her hands making a fast run for home plate, he knew he would soon be unable to say anything at all, but God, did he want her.

"Taylor." He tried to make the word come out as a warning, but it came out sounding more like wanting.

Her hands stopped a scant few inches from their intended target. Those innocent eyes met his, still showing her desire, only now there was a hint of trepidation mixed with it.

It was funny, that with all that had already transpired between them that she would be worried whether he wanted her or not. But it was right there in the deep brown depths and the slight quiver of her shoulders.

Raising his hands to caress her cheek, his thumb brushed across her lush, ripe lips. He longed to kiss away her fears and doubts. First he needed to make sure none of those fears and doubts had to do with what they both so clearly wanted.

"I want to make love to you so much, Taylor. But before we can even think about traveling down that road, I need you to be one hundred percent sure it's what you want too."

He saw a sparkle of laughter dot her eyes a moment before the word left her mouth. "No."

He couldn't believe his ears. Was she just playing with him?

"I want you to make love *with* me, not to me, Cade. I want to love you and bring you pleasure and have you do the same to me."

Her words stopped him dead in his tracks. Had he heard her correctly? *She wanted him?*

Growling, Cade pulled her up by her shoulders until she was straddling him. "Woman, you drive me insane. Do you know that?"

"Well, good. Then that makes us even, Detective." Her

hands rested on his chest. Slowly she began to caress his pectorals through the thin material of his T-shirt, then traveling lower over his rock-hard abs.

Grabbing her hands, Cade stilled her wanton exploration before she got to his erection. "Are you sure this is what you want?" The words were barely out of his mouth before she covered his lips with her own.

They tasted each other. Taylor licked his bottom lip, then dived in to flick across his teeth before meeting his tongue head on. They dueled and retreated, battling for a spot in each other's moist recesses. Finally separating, they were both breathless and panting. Their eyes locked, while their hands continued to explore each other. Cade slipped his hands under the hem of Taylor's sports bra, cupping her generous breasts. Her head fell back on a moan as his thumbs brushed and circled her hardened nipples.

Cade's shirt was quickly disposed of as Taylor tried to burrow into him. His skin was like fire and Taylor was the moth being pulled to him. His warmth, his strength. Cade made quick work of ridding Taylor of the oppressive bra and bent to take her nipple into his hot mouth. His tongue swirled and flicked the sensitive nub causing hissing and moaning to flow from Taylor's lips.

Her hands glided over the light mat of chest hair that covered Cade. Seeking out his nipples, she gently pinched them, wringing a gasp of surprise from him. He grabbed her wrists as if to push her away from her targets, but he surprised her by using his thumbs to open her palms then glided her open hands softly across his nipples forming hard peaks.

"Be gentle, Taylor."

The remorse evident in her eyes almost blocking out the passion. She whispered, "I'm sorry. I didn't mean to hurt you."

Bringing one of her palms to his lips, he placed a sweet, chaste kiss there. "You didn't hurt me. It's just that you have to be gentle with highly sensitive areas. I mean it's not like this is your first time, you should know these things."

When her eyes immediately started darting around the room like she was looking for the quickest escape route, all the air rushed from his lungs. Surely she wasn't doing this for the first time. No way would you convince him that a beautiful woman like Taylor was a virgin.

"Taylor."

Her eyes stopped searching for an exit, but they wouldn't meet his either. Tipping her chin up and holding her in place so she had no choice, but to look at him, she closed her eyes. "Taylor? This isn't your first time, is it?"

There was a slight tremble of her bottom lip before she bit down on it hard enough to draw a small amount of blood.

"Please open your eyes and look at me."

When she opened her eyes, chocolate brown pools slowly filling up and overflowing with tears greeted him.

Wiping away a fat tear as it rolled unceremoniously down her pink cheek, he whispered, "Please tell me you're not a virgin, Taylor. You weren't going to let me take that precious of a gift without telling me, were you?"

Her slight nod was barely recognizable. If he hadn't been staring so hard at her he might have missed it. But what exactly did the nod mean? Yes, she's a virgin, or yes, she was going to tell him?

"Taylor, talk to me."

"I - I'm not a virgin. But I've only done this once and it was over way before I had a chance to, um, explore anything."

Cade didn't know whether to be relieved or enraged. How

could someone take this wonderful woman's gift and not school her properly in the way of pleasure.

"Did he..." God was he really going to ask her something so personal. Too late to back out now, she was looking at him with such intensity, no doubt trying to discern exactly what it was he wanted to know. "Did he satisfy you?"

She looked as if she hadn't heard him, then her face changed to reveal a woman deep in thought. Had it been that long ago?

"Are you asking if he gave me an orgasm?"

Could the floor please open and swallow him up right now? Was he actually sitting here having a conversation about orgasms, when his last girlfriend--hell, let's just call her what she was, his ex-fiancée--told him that he was incapable of giving her an orgasm? His tongue felt thick. So he merely nodded.

"No. I mean, I don't think so. I've read a lot of books and I've talked with Lana about sex many times and she says that you'll know it if you have one. She says your whole body tingles and throbs. She even said that some people are so sensitive that they scream out from the pleasure and pain all mixed into one feeling." Taylor squirmed a little causing him to harden once again.

"Tommy was done long before I really got used to the feel of him inside me, so I'm pretty sure that I've never experienced an orgasm."

Cade knew what he had to do. The only question was *if* he would be able to do it. Everyone deserved to enjoy their sexual experiences. He was far from a minuteman. With him sex could drag on for hours if he was so inclined. With Taylor he knew he would be inclined to make it last for days. Gripping her around the waist, he stood up.

"Cade, what are you doing?"

"I'm going to show you what that dumb-ass Tommy didn't." He strode down the hallway, into his bedroom and softly deposited her on his bed.

Kneeling between her legs, he reached for the waistband of her exercise pants and slowly pulled them off. She instinctively lifted her hips so he could slide them down over her buttocks, then her legs, finally dropping them next to his bed. He sat back on his haunches and just stared at the beauty before him.

She was clad in nothing but a pair of pink lace thong panties. A small triangle of lace hid the thatch of brown curls he knew awaited him. The scent of her arousal hit him full force when she leaned back on her elbows and spread her legs, giving him a view of creamy white thighs.

The urge to dive headfirst and taste her was almost overpowering, but he held himself in check so that he didn't scare her. If the jerk that took her virginity hadn't had the time to spend loving her, he more than likely hadn't taken the time to taste her either. He could see the emotion evident in her eyes. She was a smart woman who'd admitted to reading books about sex. So she no doubt knew about the most intimate kiss possible, but the fear was there in her eyes all the same.

Reaching between her lush thighs, Cade ran his thumb over the moist center of her womanhood. His own manhood screamed to be released from its confines, but he held back. His time would come. Right now it was all about Taylor's experience and pleasure.

The lace was damp with evidence of her aroused state. When he pushed his thumb harder against her, seeking her most sensitive area, she drew in a deep breath as he ran his thumb down her nether lips then up again parting them ever so slightly so he could reach her clit. She almost cried out right then and there, but instead she bit her already abused lip.

"I want to taste you, Taylor. Right here." He punctuated his words by applying a small amount of pressure to her clit and then rolled it between his thumb and index finger.

Her dark brown eyes got even darker as passion took firm hold of her. He couldn't be sure, but he would have sworn she had just whispered the word, "Please."

He kept his eyes trained on her face for any possible movement that meant she was uncomfortable with what he was about to do. If she said "stop" or "don't," he would stop instantly. He stripped her of the small scrap of lace. When she was completely naked, he allowed his eyes to roam over her. She was exquisite, curved and molded in every enticing way a woman should be.

Generous breasts, rounded hips, slim waist. She was pleasingly plump in all the right areas. He traced his hands up her calves, over her knees to her beautiful thighs that shivered as he touched them and spread her legs. He watched her as he slowly lowered his mouth to her moist heat.

The first taste of her was almost enough to make him come in his pants again. She tasted sweet and tart like a ripened strawberry. Her head fell back the minute his lips touched hers. Relaxing into his ministrations, she lay back on the bed and spread her legs farther to give him better access.

Cade traced her silken folds and spread them wide with his fingers, flicking his tongue back and forth over her budded center. Sucking and nipping at her, his fingers continued to urge pleasure from her. His middle finger swirled around her opening, dipped in and out again.

Taylor's head was thrashing back and forth as the

sensations began to overtake her. She cried out as his finger entered her again, this time joined by a second finger. She was so tight Cade knew he would have a hard time not coming the minute he entered her sweet haven. His tongue continued to trace a path from where his fingers were eliciting pleasure from her throbbing clit.

Taylor's moans were coming faster now, and he knew she was on the verge of release. Pulling away from her, he told her, "Don't fight it, Taylor. Let it come."

And she did.

Her hands relaxed their death grip on his comforter. He went back to the most wonderful task of feasting on Taylor. Flicking his tongue across the tip of her highly sensitive, reddened nub, her cries were no doubt loud enough to wake the neighbors on the next block over. Her grip tightened again on the bed sheets as wave after wave of the highest pleasure washed over her.

Cade continued to lick the moisture from her as the tangy taste of her orgasm moistened her. She looked wonderful in the throes of orgasm. Now he was filled with a sense of longing to watch her eyes as she climaxed with him buried deep inside her.

"Cade, that ... was ... amazing." Her breathless words made his heart and his head swell. To know that he had brought her to her first climax, to know that she'd not faked her response to him one bit was almost a religious experience. He felt as if she had single-handedly handed him back his manly rights. His erection tried to stand tall and proud, but was still restrained by his clothes.

Standing, he stripped off his shorts and underwear and climbed in beside her. Taylor immediately gravitated towards his warmth. He pulled her close, allowing her to rest her head on his broad chest. Her hand played in his curls.

"Are you okay?"

"I'm wonderful. Absolutely wonderful." Lifting her head, she inquired, "Is that how it is for you guys?"

"Um, I'm not sure what you mean." Cade ran his hand through her curly hair, brushing it back so he could get a good look at her face.

"Like the Fourth of July. All fireworks and heart-pounding perfection. Is that what it feels like when guys climax?"

She had revealed to him how her climax had affected her without even realizing it.

"Well, it's different for every guy I'm sure. I..." His words were cut short when Taylor moved to straddle him.

"It's your turn, Detective." She grasped him firmly in her hand and began to pump him slowly. He felt his toes curling with the effort not to reach his climax without being inside her.

Stilling her hand, he whispered, "Taylor, I want to be inside you."

Obviously understanding the patience he was calling, she smiled down at him. "Where do you keep your condoms, Cade?"

God, he was going to lose it. "Top drawer of the nightstand." The words came out sounding like a frog had spoken instead of a fully aroused man.

Without dismounting, she reached over to the nightstand and took a green condom from the top drawer. She tore the wrapper open with her teeth and with her shaking hands tried to get the condom on.

Cade knew he was about to explode and leave himself embarrassed if she continued on the path she was on. Taking the condom from her he placed it on the tip of his penis and slowly rolled it on. Seeing that she was a little embarrassed that she hadn't been able to complete such a small feat, he caressed her cheek.

Flipping her over, so that he was in the dominant position, he brushed her hair back from her face. "It's okay." Then he brought his lips to hers so softly. He wanted her so bad, but still he waited for her to let him know she was sure about this.

"Please, Cade. Please make love to me."

Her hand reached for him, wanting to help guide him into her heated passage. He placed his hand over hers, keeping his eyes locked with Taylor's as he slid slowly into her. He was right. She was so tight he almost lost control. Moving slowly, he allowed her time to adjust to his size till he was in full to the hilt.

"Oh, my God, Cade. That feels so good."

"My sentiments exactly." When her hips surged up, he knew she wanted him to move, to show her everything he promised he would.

Sliding in and out of Taylor was the best experience Cade had ever had. He'd been about to tell her earlier that he himself had never experienced fireworks when he climaxed, but just the act of loving her was causing him to see stars.

When Taylor wrapped her legs around his hips, matching his rhythm, he took her mouth fiercely, his tongue matching each stroke of his lower half. He caught several moans that escaped from Taylor. Her nails bit into his back as her second orgasm overtook her. Taylor's screams mingled with his own. There was no doubt in Cade's mind that her nails were drawing small trickles of blood.

He was hanging on the precipice of climax, but held himself back wanting it to last for just a little bit longer.

Pushing himself up on his elbows, he watched Taylor's face as he drove into her again and again. She was so beautiful. Her little pants. Her brow slick with perspiration, eyes darkened and dilated with passion. When Cade felt her muscles clenching around him again signaling that she was near her third orgasm of the night, he quickened his pace so he could come with her.

"Oh, Cade!"

"Taylor!"

They exploded together in what Cade could only label as a mind-numbing experience. Leaning to the side of Taylor so he didn't put all his weight on her, he caressed her brow. "You know, about what you asked me earlier, I'd say yes."

Confusion creased her forehead when she looked at him, "Yes to what?"

"About guys seeing fireworks and everything when they climax." He kissed her then pulled back. "I've never felt that way before, but I saw stars and fireworks. The whole damn show."

Chuckling, she pulled him to her to indulge in one last kiss before they drifted off to sleep.

* * * *

Taylor stretched, feeling soreness in muscles she wasn't even aware that she possessed. Trying to get out of bed to head to the bathroom was going to be a feat in itself. She noticed that Cade wasn't in the bed. It disturbed her that he would just leave her in bed without telling her where he was headed, but she pushed the feelings aside.

He had been such a caring lover last night. A glance at the clock told her that it was just a few short hours ago that he'd loved her so thoroughly. Maybe he'd needed a drink or maybe he had to use the restroom.

Climbing out of bed, she moaned as her limbs protested

the movement. Cade wasn't in the bathroom. She grabbed a folded T-shirt from the top of a pile on his dresser. Surely he wouldn't mind her borrowing one of his shirts. She glanced at the shirt then did a double take as she took in the full meaning of what it said.

The front of the dark blue T-shirt read "Police Officer," while the back read, "Up against the wall and spread 'em." Her laughter filled the room. She picked up the yellow shirt that lay beneath that one. Underneath a picture of a floppy-eared dog were the words, "You give this dog a mighty big bone." Who would have guessed that Detective Cade Wills was a closet sexual innuendo junkie? The idea of it was just too hilarious for words.

Deciding on the police officer shirt, she put it on and went in search of the elusive detective. After a quick search of the living room and kitchen she decided that he could only be one other place. His office. She hated to disturb him if he was working. With everything that had happened lately, a big part of her just needed to see him and make sure no one had broken in and harmed him in any way.

When she reached his office door, she found it was cracked open just a little bit. Enough for her to see that Cade was indeed in there and that he was pacing a good hole in his carpet. She could see a large board in front of him covered in pictures of women with a bunch of little post-it notes stuck everywhere. String was tied from picture to picture as if to form some kind of trail.

Taylor remembered seeing something similar in some murder movies she had watched over the years. The detectives used them to lay out all the known information to find a link between the victims. Cade wasn't kidding when he said he lost himself in his cases sometimes, because he didn't stop pacing even after she had pushed the door open and entered the room.

He was wearing blue and purple plaid pajama bottoms that were slung low on his hips. His hair was tousled, but she was willing to bet it wasn't from sleep, but rather from his repeatedly running his agitated hands roughly through it.

She stayed by the door, but cleared her throat to let him know of her presence. He immediately stopped pacing. His eyes seemed to take in every inch of her, stopping mid-thigh, where the shirt she was wearing stopped. She hadn't bothered with any panties, but she wondered if he knew that.

He growled, then placed his palms on his desk and hung his head. "My God, Taylor." His whispered words nearly broke her heart. He sounded so forlorn, so exhausted.

Crossing the room, she stood behind him and encircled her arms about his waist. "It'll be okay, Cade." She hated that she couldn't put more conviction in her words, but she felt like he did ... at the end of her rope.

Cade turned in her arms and squeezed her to him like she was a life raft and he was drowning. Without needing any more prompting but that one hug, she raised her lips to his to assure him of her trust in his abilities. He was a good detective. He would solve this case.

Wanting to take his mind off his work and worries if only just for a little while, she dropped to her knees before him.

Grasping the sides of his pajama bottoms, she tugged them down over his erection. She had felt him last night, but had never seen him. He was magnificent. A strong powerful shaft nestled in a triangular thatch of brown curls so much like her own.

Running her tongue tentatively over the tip of his arousal, she tasted the small amount of fluid that had pooled there.

His sharp intake of breath had her pulling back thinking she might have hurt him, but the look of desire in his eyes plus the tug of his hand on her hair urging her closer had her going back to the task at hand.

He held on to her hair so lightly she barely knew it was there. He let her set the pace at first, tasting and licking her way around him. Groans and grunts escaped his lips every so often. When she felt his hand tighten in her hair she knew she was on an extremely sensitive part.

She traced the veins up and down the hardened shaft, then laved the tip of him before taking him fully in her mouth. He filled her so completely that a moan slipped out of her as well. He guided her through it, showing her the pace he liked and how to please him. She took it all in. When she slipped him out of her mouth and worked him with her hand while her mouth took root on his sac, she felt his knees give way slightly before he caught himself on the desk.

Working him faster and faster while she sucked on his sac below, she thought she heard him say the soft words, "I'm coming, Taylor."

She removed her hand and replaced it with her hot mouth as he exploded. She swallowed his salty seed and continued to lick him dry as he collapsed onto his desk. Grabbing his pajama bottoms, she pulled them back in place as she stood.

He pulled her to him and kissed her temple. "You are amazing. Do you know that?"

Taylor giggled her delight at his praise. "Well, I was inspired."

"Remind me to inspire you more often."

She kissed his neck, tasting the salty tang of his sweat. She snuggled into his embrace never wanting to let go.

"Are you having any luck?"

"With what, darling? As you can probably feel, my cock is in working order."

He was right. The hint of his arousal was already pressing against her belly. He would take her right then and there if she gave him another few seconds. But she needed to know about his progress in the case. They could never have a real relationship if they didn't solve it.

She had read too many times about how people misjudged their feelings for someone when they were in a stressful life or death situation. What they once saw as love turned out to be some sort of adrenaline rush. She so hoped that wasn't what was going on between her and Cade, but in order for her to be sure, they had to catch this guy and see where that left their feelings.

"I meant about the case. I knew you were a sex junkie." She pulled from his embrace and lightly slapped his shoulder.

He rubbed his shoulder pretending she had seriously wounded him. "What do you mean sex junkie? I'm not the one giving amazing oral sex to a man in his office at," he looked over at the clock on his wall above a picture of a younger version of himself, "three-thirty in the morning."

She smiled as the sarcastic remark jumped to her lips. "Well, I would hope you weren't giving oral pleasure to a guy at any time of the day. That would severely undermine my judgment of you."

"Smart aleck. Now tell me what you mean."

"I meant this T-shirt and the other ones in your room. They all had some sort of sexual innuendo on them. I didn't know you had it in you."

He sat in the black leather chair and pulled her down on his lap. "I don't. They're presents from my brother, Kacey.

He has this idea that I don't have enough fun in my life, so he sends me all these shirts. Even my sheet sets are presents from him, including the moon and stars set. Which reminds me, you still haven't told me how you knew about them."

She tried to find something else they could talk about besides that. She didn't want to scare him off now that they had become intimate. "I saw a shirt one time that you should get and put in your collection."

"Oh really, what shirt would that be?" His hand moved to cup her breast through the thin material. Her nipples budding under his touch.

"It said 'Sixty-eight, you do me and I'll owe you one.'"

His hand stilled and his face became an unreadable mask.

"What? What's the matter, Cade?"

Shaking his head, as if trying to rid himself of an evil demon, he said, "I had that shirt. When Laura left me, she took it with her."

Now it was Taylor's turn to shake her head venomously. "Who's Laura?" The stricken look that invaded his eyes was almost enough to make her burst out in tears for his pain.

"She was my fiancée. She left me over a year ago. Said she found someone who could please her more and she took the shirt with her. It wasn't until a few months later that I found out just how much that shirt fit her."

His hand tightened on her thigh, then balled into a fist.

"What do you mean it 'fit her'?"

"Well, it became abundantly clear to me that she *owed* a lot of people if you get my meaning."

Taylor entwined her fingers with his as the meaning of his words sank in. Laura had slept around with other guys while she was engaged to Cade. *What a bitch!* She caressed the back of his neck with her free hand trying to soothe the savage beast that had started to rear its ugly head at the mention of his ex-fiancée's name.

"I'm sorry." There didn't seem to be a whole lot she could say in the face of his confession. It had taken a lot for him to trust that information to her. She laid her head on his shoulder and gave him the best comfort she could. Cade's scent enveloped her as she drifted off to sleep once again.

Chapter Ten

Taylor couldn't be sure exactly what it was that woke her. She couldn't remember having any observer dreams, or any bad dreams for that matter, but her mind seemed to be preoccupied with a picture of some kind that she just couldn't seem to get a firm grasp on.

Slowly moving out of the bed so she wouldn't wake Cade, she slipped on the shirt that had been discarded when he carried her back to bed. Their lovemaking had been slow and sensual. He had brought her to several glorious climaxes before he allowed his own.

Cade was an amazing man. Taylor knew if she wasn't careful she would fall completely and hopelessly in love with him. Staring down at his face, lost in silent slumber, he reminded her of the young boy she had seen him as in her vision.

The pull to crawl back in bed and kiss him awake was strong. But the need to figure out the picture that was at the tip of her subconscious was stronger. Silently she left the bedroom and headed towards Cade's office. Her feet seemed to have a mind of their own. She couldn't remember consciously making the decision to go there.

The pictures of beautiful dead girls littered Cade's desktop. She picked up a few, and then felt her hand dig down beneath the pile of pictures and retrieve a brown envelope. Grabbing a pair of scissors out of a black desk organizer full of pens and pencils, Taylor went to the kitchen and sat down at the dining room table.

Dumping out the contents of the envelope, Taylor gasped as her name stared back at her. The envelope was filled with the photos taken of the patterns and words written in blood. Her name stood staring at her in big bold letters. She picked up the picture of her name and set it aside then picked up the next picture and began deftly cutting out the patterns and letters that appeared in each photo.

As if her hands had been possessed they flew through the task before them. When she was finally done cutting, she began to piece together the pictures to form a pattern. It quickly became all too clear what the killer had been trying to tell her all along.

When her hands stopped moving and she finally felt like they were her hands again, she stared in awe at the sight before her.

The head of a lion with his mouth open in a fierce growl, surrounded by vines intertwining to read "Circus Anyone."

"Whatcha doing?"

Taylor screamed and fell off the side of the chair, smacking her bottom hard on the cool tile floor.

Cade was at her side in a flash, his hands caressing her tender flesh. "Are you okay? I didn't mean to scare you."

"I'm fine." Taylor pulled herself back up into the chair. "I was... I think I know what the symbols are." Taylor pointed to the makeshift puzzle she had put together and heard Cade's sharp intake of breath.

His hand ran through his sleep tousled hair. "When did you figure this out?"

"Just now. I woke up and had this picture in my head. My hands seemed like they were bewitched, almost like they couldn't cut it out fast enough."

Taylor watched as Cade bent over the kitchen table to get a better look at the picture forming before him. She could see by the set of his shoulders that he was holding back the urge to jump for joy at the thought they could catch the killer and end all these deaths.

When his eyes met hers she saw his relief, but his eyes seemed to be trying to communicate something else, something she couldn't read or understand.

"You stay here. I'm going to go take a shower and get dressed. I'll get the boys together and we will finish this."

Taylor knew now what that look had been. It was the cop mode kicking in. He was going to keep her out of this. He didn't want her to be involved. Well that was just too damned bad. She was involved, more than she'd ever wanted to be, but involved just the same.

Something still didn't feel quite right. Why all of a sudden would she immediately know what the scribbles on the wall meant? Was the killer tired of waiting for her to figure it out on her own? Was he ready to meet her face to face? Was it a set up for the police, for Cade?

Too many unanswered questions and Cade going into his He-Man detective disposition inspired anger to boil up inside her. "I want to go. I have a right to be there."

Cade's hand sliced through the air silencing her. "This is police business, Taylor. You will stay here and stay safe." He pointed his finger at her then towards the ground punctuating every word. "I will go get the bad guy. Okay?"

He gave her a quick peck on the cheek then left the room. He seemed to think the master had spoken and no one better dare go against what he said.

Well, Mr. High-and-mighty, I am not some child you can push around. I will not be ordered to stay put like some animal.

She knew it was wrong of her to feel hurt that Cade would try to keep her out of this. He was only trying to protect her. Any sensible woman would just say 'okay' and be done with the whole thing, but she couldn't shake this feeling that she was the one who was supposed to take down the killer. It was like the Night Stalker wanted her to be the one to stop him.

Taylor went down the hall to tell Cade that she was going. Even if she just sat in the squad car, she had to be there. She laughed to herself when she realized that Cade was singing in the shower. So much tension had just been lifted off him that he was carefree enough to sing. Taylor wished she felt the same way.

A burning, stabbing feeling shot through her gut, doubling her over in pain. She grabbed the dresser to keep from falling over. The whispered voice spoke to her, the sound resounding in her head over and over again. "Come to me, Taylor. Come to me."

When the pain subsided a strange sensation tingled throughout her body. A foggy, drugged feeling filled her head. She felt as if a rope had been tied around her waist and was tugging her towards the door. Mindlessly, she dressed and grabbed Cade's keys off the dresser. About to leave the house, something held her back. Struggling against the mental fog, she managed to scrawl, "Gone to get him, Taylor" on a scrap of paper and left it on the kitchen table. Her need to communicate with Cade satisfied, she gave up the futile struggle to resist the compulsion and left the house.

* * * *

Cade knew something was wrong the minute he got out of the shower. He knew he'd been too overbearing, ordering Taylor to stay here while he went out and closed this case. But he knew Taylor being there at the scene would cloud his judgment. He would be too worried about her safety to concentrate on his own or that of his other officers. Hopefully she would understand that he was only looking out for her.

He'd known instantly where the killer had been hiding the minute he saw the puzzle on his kitchen table. As a child he had loved going to see the traveling circus. Every year it came through town with its lights, animals and the Ferris wheel. *Circus Anyone* was full of the most spectacular sights: lions, tigers, a bearded fat lady, conjoined twins, a contortionist, everything imaginable. When the zoo opened and then bigger circuses like Barnum and Bailey came to town, they seemed to just disappear.

They were now just a forgotten part of the past. The remnants of Circus Anyone lay at the outskirts of town, the cages abandoned, the whole place deserted.

Toweling his hair dry, he walked into the kitchen to tell Taylor that the officers were going to meet him about a mile from the location so they could decide on a plan. He stopped dead in his tracks. She wasn't there. He looked around the kitchen, calling her name. He checked his office. The living room. Nothing. He checked out the front door. Sure enough his truck was gone.

She was gone.

He headed to his bedroom, grabbing his cell on the way when he saw the hastily scrawled note on the table. Cade crumpled the note up and threw it across the room. "Damn fool woman!" He darted to his room, dressing and calling the Chief at the same time to give him the news.

* * * *

Taylor felt the foggy, drugged feeling start to subside as she looked out the truck window. She couldn't remember consciously making the decision to come here alone. Had the killer taken over her mind this time? She was parked inside the entrance to the abandoned lot of Circus Anyone. The sign overhead was deteriorating and hanging kind of lopsided. A slight breeze caused the wooden sign to sway and creak. The quiet was eerie. A chill raced down Taylor's back.

"Okay, you forced me to come here alone, you son of a bitch. What now?" Taylor whispered into the emptiness. She ought to head straight back to Cade and safety. That would be the smart thing to do. But the feeling grew in her that if she did, she would bring the danger with her. Somehow she knew that the only way to solve this was to go by herself. She had learned to trust her visions. She had to trust this feeling. It was all she had to go on to keep Cade and the rest of the world safe.

"God, please keep me safe."

She stepped from the car, closing the door silently so she wouldn't attract any attention. Every small sound was amplified. Her shoes crunched on the gravel. Her breathing sounded like a marathon runner. Her heart beat loudly in her ears. Although it was light outside, the place gave her the creeps. The cages she passed reminded her of the dream where someone was chasing her.

Was that her fate? To be eaten alive by some lion in one of these cages?

No, she wouldn't think like that. Nothing had lived in these cages for years. The stench of rotting feces and the sight of dead vegetation assured her of that. She noticed a dead bird lying next to a cage that had the words *the amazing wolf boy* written on it. She couldn't tell whether it died of natural causes. The decay of the body had progressed so much that only bones and a few feathers remained.

Taylor felt the hair prickle at the back of her neck. Every

muscle in her body tensed when she heard her name whispered on the breeze. Goose bumps raised on her arms and legs. She knew it was crazy, but suddenly she heard a voice in her head screaming, "Run!" It sounded like Cade's voice telling her to run. Of course, at this moment she didn't care if it was God Almighty telling her to get a move on, Taylor knew it was time to move.

She took off running in the opposite direction from where she felt the killer was watching her. If only this psychic power she had came when she needed it and not when it felt like it. When she heard pounding feet behind her, she forced her legs to speed up. It hadn't been that long since she'd been running with Lana, but her muscles were protesting the effort. Her mind kept encouraging her that everything would be okay, that she just had to run faster. Farther. When she noticed a building behind what used to be the main circus tent, she darted for the open door.

The musty scent from her dream the other night nearly knocked her off her feet. She froze, realizing that this was where *he* stayed. His room was just a few paces from where she stood. Her mind reeled. She was trapped. He would find her and she was going to die in this rundown old boiler room. That had to be where she was standing. Pipes hissed and released steam all around her. Her mind screamed for her to get out of this place.

She jumped when the door slammed shut behind her, leaving her in total darkness. Her hands felt along the wall. Something slimy and moist slid through her fingers. Taylor pulled Cade's keys from out of her pocket, remembering that he had one of those small key lights. It didn't give her much light since it was meant to merely show you the keyhole so you didn't scratch up your car door, but it was somewhat comforting just to know that she wasn't in complete and total darkness.

* * * *

Cade drove his Harley to the spot where all the officers were to meet. He wanted to head straight for the Circus Anyone compound, but his chief had insisted he keep his head on straight. Cade wanted to shove his fist down the chief's throat right then and there and if they hadn't been on the telephone, he probably would have. He was capable of doing his job and protecting Taylor. He had to be. Her life depended on him now.

Without Taylor he would be lost, but she had knowingly gone against him and walked right into the lion's den. Given her dreams of this place and the power the killer was exerting to get to her, she should have known better. Cade didn't know if he would be able to forgive her for scaring him to death because he could lose another person he loved. He damn well was going to make sure that she knew his feelings for her when this was all said and done.

Yes, he did love her, so he would probably eventually be able to forgive her. If she lived. Understanding her, now that was probably a lost cause.

What man understood women anyways?

Ever since he lost his best friend and his brother, he made it a point not to hold things back, to always make sure the people in his life knew how he felt about them so that there would be no regrets later on if there was an accident or death. But he hadn't been able to open up to Taylor, to tell her that he had fallen madly, hopelessly in love with her. He could only hope that she felt the same way about him.

"Wills! Get over here." Chief Dugan bellowed over the group of officers in a circle around the hood of the police cruiser with Police Chief stamped across the sides.

Cade parked his motorcycle and reached the group in

record time. They already had a diagram laid out for the abandoned circus. Positions were marked for points of penetration. Cade wanted to just rush in full force and take this guy down, but he was glad that someone was thinking clearly. He didn't want Taylor to be injured.

"Now, we know that Ms. Cole is already here because of Wills' vehicle." No one dared breathe, let alone speak as the chief went on. "We have no evidence at this time that she is in the custody of the perp, but for her sake let's assume she is. We need our 'A' game, gentlemen. The perp may be armed and dangerous. Your orders are to take him alive if at all possible, but if you happen to kill the son of bitch you won't hurt my feelings any." The officers all smiled and glanced around to see if everyone was on the same page. "Everyone to your designated entry points."

Cade felt the chief's death grip on his forearm as he turned to mount his bike. "Wills, I need your full attention here."

Cade forced himself to stare into his chief's, his friend's eyes, "Trust me, you have it, sir."

At the chief's nod of approval they all raced towards the dilapidated circus, intending to bring down a serial killer and save an innocent woman. Cade hoped like hell that no one screwed this up. Especially him.

* * * *

The door out of the building had been locked, forcing Taylor to look for another way out. Her heart pounding like a jackhammer, she passed a few empty rooms, and reached a door that she *knew* led to the Night Stalker's lair. Sprawled on the floor to the side was the body of the man she had seen in her dream. She guessed he had been strangled.

Shining the thin beam of the key light around, she

couldn't see any other way out. Taking a deep breath, she pushed the door open slowly. She exhaled sharply in relief when she saw that he wasn't behind the door waiting for her like he was in her dream.

Everything seemed just as her dream had been. The moth-eaten blanket lay forgotten on a thin, worn-out mattress. The table was piled high with pictures of different women. Some were covered in red paint, others were slashed to pieces. Taylor noticed several pictures of her. Her smiling. Laughing with Cade in Margie's Diner. There were even pictures of her running from the guy at the library.

"Do you like them?"

Fear gripped her insides and she nearly jumped out of her skin when she heard his voice. She'd known he was around, felt him near. But knowing he was standing right behind her, and that this room didn't appear to have any exits other than the door he was now blocking was terrifying. *Stay strong, confident. Brave.*

"They're very nice." She didn't want to turn around. After all this time of seeing him with a mask on, she wasn't sure if she really wanted to see the face of her killer before she died.

"You're not like the rest of them."

She heard his feet shuffle across the threshold and the door squeak shut. The air in the room seemed to thin and her chest was fighting to draw in a normal breath.

"Why did you kill them all?" Her hand brushed aside her pictures to see a picture of Evita. The memory of finding out her neighbor's twin sister had been murdered assailed her. The devastation that Consuela felt, that her whole family would feel. "What could all these women possibly have done to deserve to die like that?"

"My reasons are my own. They were no innocent

victims!" He stated the last with a sneer, but his voice remained nothing more than a whisper in the still air.

Taylor closed her eyes expecting him to strike out at her at any moment. When she felt his breath on her neck, she sucked in a gulp of air, preparing herself for the fatal blow.

"I would never hurt you, Taylor. You're not like them." His hand gestured to the pictures before her.

Taylor noticed that he wore black gloves with the fingers cut off. The parts of his fingers that showed were badly scarred. Some were even missing the fingernails. His hand grazed her arm then slowly caressed her forearm up to her bicep. Taylor's head began to swim. She felt like she was on a ship rocking in the ocean. Her eyesight blurred and she waited for the darkness to take her.

Chapter Eleven

Taylor headed down the dark wood-paneled hallway towards the sound of male laughter. Several pictures covered the walls. Pictures of guys washing cars, several group photos. Beta Theta Pi was engraved on the small plaque that graced the bottom of the frames. She figured she must be inside some fraternity house.

Taylor knew she was in a vision. A vision that could only be from the Night Stalker, so she tried to take it all in, memorizing every door she passed, every photo on the wall. When she came to a door that led off to what could only be a living room, she passed through the doorway.

There was a nice looking young man standing before two peers seated on a red suede couch. The two seated were dressed in matching khaki dress slacks that were severely starched and creased, white shirts with red sweaters wrapped around their shoulders proudly displaying the Greek letters that represented their fraternity name.

"Please guys, I really need to be in this fraternity."

The young man standing in front of them was dressed in dark-colored sweats. His face was angular with some boyish charm, a dimple lanced through his left cheek as he begged the fraternity brothers to let him in. His blond hair was mussed and some strands were plastered to the side of his face. He looked like he had just finished running a marathon.

Laughter rang out yet again. "I'm sorry, man, but you just couldn't hack it. If you can't make it through Hell Week, you can't be in our fraternity. You chickened out the second day."

"I know, but I can do this. I have to do this. Can you please give me another chance?"

The boy with dark brown hair stood and turned to leave without another word to the boy Taylor's intuition told her had to be the Stalker. She noticed he didn't have any scarring on his hands yet.

Once the young man had gone, the one that was left spoke. "David, listen, you just don't have what it takes to be a Beta Theta Pi brother. There are other fraternities here; try pledging them."

"Please, Shaun. I'm willing to do anything you guys ask of me. My father was a brother here. I have to get in." David wrung his hands nervously.

"I'll tell you what, David, let me discuss it with Chris and the other brothers and see what we can figure out." Shaun seemed to look upon David with sympathy, almost as if he cared what David was going through.

Shaun left the room, leaving David to pace and ponder his fate with the fraternity. The hands on the clock sitting on the wooden mantle above an impressive fireplace swirled until they showed that almost an hour had passed. Shaun and Chris returned to the room. David immediately stood from his perch on the armrest of the red couch.

"We've decided that if you will do one more stunt for us and succeed in your mission, you will be able to finish out Hell Week with the other pledges."

Relief was evident on David's face.

Funny how she had gone to calling him David so fast. It seemed to suit this young man that stood before her, more than the Night Stalker label. Maybe because this was him before he became a murderer.

"What is it? I'll do anything you ask." David's eyes filled with unshed tears. Taylor swore she could hear his heartbeat speed up at the thought of being let in to the fraternity.

"Your mission, if you choose to accept it, is to break in to Alpha Gamma Delta's sorority house and bring back the Greek banner that hangs in the pledge room on the top floor. If you succeed you can once again join your brethren in pledging. If you fail to retrieve it or are caught by the house mother you must leave us be and never darken our door again." The fraternity brothers seemed to share a slight look between them before David spoke.

"I will not fail my brothers. I will make you proud to accept me back into the fold." David bowed and walked backwards never taking his eyes off the two boys until he had reached the door leading outside.

Taylor followed him, glancing back to see the boys laughing and slapping each other on the back. Obviously something wasn't as it seemed. She followed David across the campus, taking in the fact that no one acknowledged him or said anything to him, but they sure seemed to start whispering to each other as soon as he passed by them.

Several big guys wearing lettermen jackets walked by, shoving David out of the way. The girls that were following them laughed as David nearly fell to the ground.

"Watch where you're going, psycho!"

David merely laughed uncomfortably and scrubbed his hand across the back of his neck. "Sorry guys, my fault. Must not have been paying attention to where I was going."

The boys moved off laughing and joking with each other. The words "crazy" and "lunatic" were the only things she could catch from their conversation.

David hurried into a building and ran up the flight of

stairs. Taylor stayed with him, not wanting to lose him. He pulled a key from his pocket and unlocked the first door he came to.

Upon entering, Taylor noticed that even though there was a second bed in the room, it appeared no one stayed on that side of the room. He rummaged through his closet and produced a pair of black sweats, complete with a hooded shirt. He dug in a box that was on the floor of the closet and came back with a black ski mask.

"I knew you would come in handy one day." David told the mask and a chill entered Taylor's heart at the thought that one day that mask would conceal his face from the innocent victims he killed.

He took his shirt off revealing a sculpted upper body with strongly muscled abs. His skin was bronzed to perfection. He slipped his hands inside his waistband and removed his pants, revealing that he was totally naked underneath. Taylor turned her head away abruptly, but couldn't help but sneak a peek. David crossed in front of her and went into the small bathroom located off to the side of the closet.

Her eyes were riveted to his backside as she took in the picture. He was every woman's dream come true. Toned back, nice tight ass. Everything about him oozed sexuality and hinted at a most pleasant ride and yet he had an aura about him that screamed the words sad and lonely.

She watched as David started the water in the shower, testing the temperature. He climbed into the stall and pulled the shower curtain shut, cutting off her view. Although his form could be made out, it was all a blur. She turned to look around his room taking in the fact that it was immaculately clean. A place for everything and everything in its place seemed to be David's motto. For a boy in college he was awfully anal about cleanliness.

The sound of moaning had her turning to face the cloudy figure in the shower. She could make out movement at his groin area. A loud moan erupted from David's lips as what Taylor could only guess was his own hand pumping his cock. The one she found most delightfully gorgeous only a moment ago. She could hear the harsh breathing and groans. A part of her yearned to pull back the curtain and take a peek at him pleasuring himself, but another tried to remind her why she was here. It was becoming harder and harder to reconcile this handsome young man with the killer she had come to know.

"God, Taylor, when will you come for me? Uh, oh, God, I'm coming for you, now!"

Taylor gasped at her name and the words that he said. He told her that he was coming for her once before. *Was this what he meant?* And how did he know who she was now? She had to have been hearing something that the Stalker wanted her to hear, not what was really said at this time.

She watched as his body slumped against the wall sated from his own hand. She walked to the bedroom and sat on his bed trying to figure things out.

When he finally exited the bathroom he was fully clothed in the black sweats he had pulled from the closet. He set the alarm clock sitting next to the bed for midnight and lay down on the bed next to where Taylor sat.

"Soon I shall have you, Taylor, and I will make you feel as good as you make me feel." His whispered words skated through her head as he drifted off to sleep.

When the alarm finally went off several hours later, Taylor still hadn't figured out why she was stuck here. She tried to walk out of the room while he slept, but there seemed to be an invisible wall barring her exit. So she had looked through his things, almost hyperventilating when she found a notebook with her name doodled all through it. Nothing but her name.

Taylor didn't know why or how for that matter, but even back then he seemed to know they were destined to meet.

She came across his journal and read in it about him having observer dreams. About the whole town thinking he and his mom were both psychos because of their abilities. He came to college in hopes of a fresh start, but after falling asleep in class one day and totally freaking out from witnessing a murder in his dreams, everyone had found out about his difference.

Now he was "psycho" to everyone. No one wanted to be his friend. No one. Except Shaun. He had showed him friendship and hadn't cared what others said about him.

When David finally pulled himself awake and turned off the alarm, Taylor knew that a part of her heart could relate to what David had gone through, because it was something she had gone through every day since the accident. Slipping his feet into some running shoes, he snuck out of his dorm room and crept quietly down the stairs. Obviously he didn't want to make anyone aware that he was out of his room. Taylor followed close behind, wondering if she would ever find out what happened to make such a seemingly nice boy turn so evil.

It took nearly thirty minutes to reach the Alpha Gamma Delta sorority house. Another twenty to break in without causing much damage or noise. They entered through the back door which led into a very beautiful gourmet kitchen with an island. The counters were covered with dark brown and black marble. The kitchen floor was done in white slate tile. David found the spiral staircase that led to what she hoped was the upstairs pledge room. Even though she knew she was merely an observer her heart was racing with adrenaline as if she was the one breaking and entering.

The staircase ended at the beginning of a long hallway. The walls were painted a creamy yellow, reminding Taylor of a beautiful sunny day. Pictures covered the walls like in the fraternity. Girls having fun, girls in the kissing booth charging a dollar for a kiss. Washing cars. Then several rows of sorority pictures. Something in one of the pictures made Taylor stop dead in her tracks.

A woman, looking much like a younger version of her mother, was poised in one of the pictures off to the side with another older woman. But it couldn't be, her mother had never been in a sorority, she would have told her something like that.

Wasn't being in a sorority something to be proud of?

Taylor thought she heard giggling coming from the door they had just passed, but that was silly, it was almost one o'clock in the morning. David must have heard it too because he paused and listened intently. He obviously decided he was hearing things because he continued down the hall.

After passing two other closed doors, they finally reached an open one. The Alpha Gamma Delta banner hung over the fireplace along with two small tea light candles that were lit on either side of the banner. They entered the room and stood staring at the banner and the lit candles for what seemed like forever.

Suddenly the room grew brighter and the soft sound of a door clicking in place made David and Taylor turn towards the entrance. Nine girls stood inside the room against the now closed door. They looked to be about eighteen to twenty years old and each held a lit pillar candle. Taylor noticed immediately that none of them were wearing any clothes.

It took a moment for Taylor to recognize that each of the girls were familiar to her. They were younger versions than she had known, but each of them had been one of the Stalker's victims. She heard David's rapid intake of breath and it was hard not to notice the tent that had been created within his sweatpants. That little bit of information didn't seem to pass the girls up either. They giggled and Taylor knew instantly that they had been set up. Or rather David had been.

"Um, look what we have here, girls. A dream man here to make all our dreams come true." The sleek blonde that Taylor knew as his last victim set her candle down on the dresser standing next to the door. The other girls followed suit.

David's gulp seemed to reverberate around the room as he watched the blonde's hand travel over first one breast and then the other. She squeezed her breast and brought the nipple to her lips, taking it into her mouth and suckling it. David flinched as one of the other girls leaned over and slipped the blonde's other nipple into her mouth.

The girls each started touching the other. First breasts, then getting bolder and running their hands down each other's bodies to slip between wet folds and caress each other's swollen lips. David's jaw nearly came unhinged as the girl Taylor could only guess was a younger Evita got down on her knees in front of the blonde and began to lick her slit. No one said a word. Just stood touching each other and watching David's reaction.

Taylor was dumbfounded. As far as she could see this was any man's fantasy, surely this was not what he killed them for. For a little bit of sexual torture.

David's hand had strayed to the front of his sweats to caress the length of himself through the fabric. His eyes kept floating from one to another trying to see everything, not wanting to miss anything. Taylor was riveted to her spot, never having seen so many people going at it, and never having watched girls with other girls. She hated the fact that she felt moisture seeping from her own slit especially from watching Evita lick the blonde's pussy. The blonde's head was thrown back as if she was lost in oblivion with Evita sucking and licking to her heart's content.

When the blonde opened her eyes and fastened them on David she whispered, "Let me see it, stud."

David complied immediately, pulling his hardened cock from inside his sweats. The drops of pre-cum were sliding down the sides as he stroked it slowly. Taylor didn't know what to look at or if she should be looking at all. Here before her stood a killer who wasn't a killer yet stroking a massive hard-on with nine victims who weren't victims yet touching and licking and even fingering each other.

Should she be aroused? Should she be appalled? Taylor didn't know. She just knew that she couldn't *not* look.

"That's a big cock you have there." Taylor guessed that was the second victim talking. She was watching David masturbating while driving three of her fingers into victim number four. Her strokes followed his and number four's juices were running over her hand.

"Would you like to play with us, big boy?" Evita had stopped licking the blonde long enough to ask.

David swallowed several times before he whispered, "Hell yeah."

The girls all came at him at once. They pulled him over to a chair that was tucked into the corner across from the fireplace. Taylor watched as they sat him in it and took turns climbing on top of him and riding his thick, rigid staff. The girl's moans were loud enough to wake the dead or maybe they just seemed that way to Taylor.

She watched as David's penis became saturated in the girls' come. While one was riding him, the other girls were taking turns with each other. It had become one big orgy. Still Taylor couldn't figure out how this would make him want to kill them, but she continued to watch for any little thing that was wrong.

Finally, she saw it.

There were two girls grabbing something from under the chair. Rope. The girls talked him into turning around and sitting on his knees in the chair facing the back. They caressed his back while continuing to stroke his stiff rod. They tied his hands to the back chair legs and his feet to the front chair legs.

Victim number one had her head between his body and the chair and was sucking him deep into her mouth. Taylor could see as the girls moved to the side that they had stripped him bare. His ass stuck in the air and his hard penis and swollen scrotum hung between his legs. He looked back over his shoulder with a look of complete lust.

Taylor noticed victim number eight, the one she had seen with the baby, had moved to a closet door. When she swung it open, disbelief followed closely by rage clouded over David's face. There stood the frat boys who had sent him on this mission. And they had friends. Five altogether exited the closet. It wasn't until David saw the video camera that he strained against his bindings. They had taped it. For the entire world to see.

And yet Taylor was still confused. Most guys would have bragging rights when it came to getting it on with nine women at once. When she caught a glimpse of what the dark-haired frat boy, Chris, carried in his hand, she thought she knew why David had freaked out. A huge, purple dildo hung from his hand. Another fraternity brother had a bottle of KY Jelly in his hand. Surely they didn't intend to....

The thought died away when the boys reached David. He fought against his restraints, so much so Taylor could see he was drawing blood. The girls had tied him up tight. The boy that Taylor thought showed sympathy towards David earlier in the day took the bottle of lube and poured it down between David's cheeks. But instead of grabbing the dildo, Shaun undid his pants and crammed his hardened dick into David's ass.

She heard David cry out in pain followed by some very choice curse words. David tried to buck against the ropes, but it seemed to just fuel the frat boy's lust. She realized now that lust was what she had seen in Shaun's eyes earlier. Not sympathy. He raped David while the girls watched and the frat boys cheered and urged him on. David cried and screamed. Taylor's heart broke, almost forgetting that she was merely an onlooker, she tried to get the guy off of David. But her hands passed right through him.

The frat boys continued to tape David's humiliation and even took their turns with the girls. When Shaun finally came, he pulled out and came all over David's back. David had stopped fighting long before Shaun was finished. Silently sobbing, his wrists bled and Taylor noticed that blood leaked down the back of his legs too.

"What are we going to do with him now? Someone has to untie him." Evita spoke up after everyone was finished with their fun.

Shaun reached down and untied one of David's legs from the chair. David roared with anger and kicked out, knocking the rapist back into the dresser holding the candles. The candles fell and instantaneously caught the drapes on fire. The girls began screaming and the boys panicked. They tried to put the fire out with their shirts but they only succeeded in making the fire grow. David was fighting to get out of the chair.

Chaos erupted in the room. The girls tried to help put the fire out by hitting it with some throw pillows from the floor, but when they caught on fire too they screamed louder. The room was slowly being engulfed in flames. The flames jumped from curtains to pillows to the carpet. The girls ran out of the room yelling that they needed a fire extinguisher. The guys ran out after the girls steadily adjusting their clothing, leaving David tied to the chair.

Taylor heard the commotion in the hallway and looked out just in time to see something she never expected to see.

Chapter Twelve

Taylor couldn't believe what was occurring right in front of her. Nine naked girls trying to throw robes on while five boys tried desperately to explain not only why they were in the sorority house, but why they were half nude and that there was a fire in the pledge room to the rudely awakened house mother who had too close of a resemblance to Taylor's mother for her comfort.

"Mother Cole, please listen. There's a fire in the pledge room, we have to call nine-one-one, get a fire extinguisher or something. Anything. It's spreading fast!" Evita had to scream above all the others that were panicking now as flames licked past Taylor's legs out into the hallway.

Taylor stood with her mouth wide open, not fully comprehending what was going on. Her mother was these sorority girls' house mother. How could that be?

Nothing seemed to slow the chaos that was happening around her until the ear splitting, bone-tingling scream pierced the air.

David!

Taylor turned to see David struggling to get himself loose from the chair. Flames seared the hair off his legs, singeing skin along with it. Taylor's mother appeared in the doorway with a fire extinguisher in hand. Taylor wasn't sure where she got it, but she was sure glad her mom came to the rescue.

David continued to wrestle with his bonds. The legs of the chair broke, finally giving out from the weight above and the fire below. Aiming the extinguisher at the base of the fire, her mother began to spray, but it was too late to stop the blaze. The flames seemed to laugh up at her as she tried to control the fire.

"Who's in here? Girl's, who's left in here?" Her mother screamed to make herself heard. David's screams became more persistent as Taylor watched helplessly while his body was engulfed in flames. When the reply came Taylor felt as if her stomach would fall straight through the floor.

"It's the freak!"

Taylor didn't know which one had said the words, but she knew the second her mother realized who she was so desperately trying to save. Her mother paused for the briefest second and made eye contact with David. His screams ceased for that moment, when he realized that she couldn't help him. Maybe wouldn't, was what he thought. The sick feeling in the pit of her stomach got worse when the craziest idea popped into her head ... maybe her mother and father's death hadn't been an accident.

* * * *

Cade didn't know what he'd do if anything happened to Taylor. God, what he wouldn't give to go back to that moment when he told her she couldn't go with him to make the arrest. He would have *made* her go with him. That way at least he'd have known she was in a squad car safe with another officer looking out for her.

He had his gun trained in front of him, sweeping from side to side, looking for any movement among the shadows. His nostrils flared as he caught wind of what smelled like rotting animal feces. He brushed his free hand across his nose trying to shut out the offensive smell.

There were empty cages where animals were displayed when he was a child. Lions and tigers used to traipse inside the cages looking as if they would eat any kid alive who dared get too close. Large orangutans used to swing from bar to bar along the top of the cage. He could almost hear the animals now, roaring and grunting.

When he saw the small shack of a building before him, something in his gut tensed. *Is Taylor in there? Is she okay or have I already lost her?* Cade couldn't tolerate the thought of the Night Stalker claiming Taylor's life. Of her beauty and light gone from the world. From his life. His stomach seized up and he retched right there on the ground.

"Are you okay, Detective Wills?"

Cade heard the whispered inquiry, but he took a minute to pull himself together before answering. The older detective's hand rested on his back to steady him.

He shook his head and replied, "I'm fine, just must have been something I ate." He knew it was a lie and the other officer obviously did too judging from the sympathy in his eyes.

Cade had never made his and Taylor's relationship public knowledge but still everyone seemed to know. Every cop on the scene had looked at him with compassion while they discussed their plans.

Could they really tell how he felt about Taylor just by looking at him?

The officer patted him on the back. He nodded towards Cade, "Do you think she might be in here, sir?"

God, I hope not! "Yeah, she might be. But our killer might be in there with her. We have to take it slow."

Cade saw the officer's nod and reached for the door.

* * * *

Taylor seemed to flash forward in what she saw. It was like watching a movie and pushing fast forward on the machine. She saw in a blur the fire department arriving before the whole building was lost. Firefighters pulling David from the fire, nearly eighty percent of his body burned. Her mother stood beside the girls as they were questioned about the cause of the fire. Her mom hugged Evita to her chest and whispered words of encouragement.

They watched as David was loaded into the back of a nearby ambulance. Taylor crawled into the ambulance and sat watching as the paramedic worked on getting an IV started. Taylor saw that her mother's attention stayed glued to the ambulance until they were out of sight.

Focusing back on David, Taylor noticed his face was burned badly and the smell of burnt flesh was enough to make her want to heave. His eyes were closed and she thought he might even be dead, then his eyes flew open and he screamed out one word. The sound of it would forever remain with her, "Taylor!"

The vision fast forwarded again to David lying in a hospital bed covered in gauze from head to toe. He looked like a mummy from some ancient Egyptian tomb. He lay there, whispering her name over and over again while staring out the window. Her heart broke to see what he had gone through, to know what those college boys had done, and the girls.... She understood now why he insisted they weren't innocent. They had played their role as well.

Taylor jumped when she heard people enter David's room. When she saw that it was the ones responsible for all of this she had to restrain herself from flying across the room to tell them exactly what she thought of them. But that would prove useless just like her attempts at saving him from being raped.

"Hey, Psyc ... I mean David." The boy Taylor remembered as Chris from the fraternity house stepped closer to the bed. David turned to look at them. The ones who had raped him and left him to be burned alive.

"The police are going to be coming by to ask you some questions. We thought it might be better if you knew what we told them so our stories could match up." David's eyes narrowed as he stared at the boy who had helped take his life from him. "We told them we were doing a panty raid and the girls must have heard us and got scared when they saw us. They dropped the candles and the fire burned out of control before we had a chance to put it out."

David mumbled something that even she didn't hear. The bewilderment on the boy's face was evident as he leaned closer trying to make out what David had said. Taylor leaned in as well.

"You die first." Those three little whispered words made Chris jump back away from David. Taylor saw that the boy hadn't misinterpreted what David had said, he took it for the threat it was.

"What did he say, Chris?" Shaun asked impatiently.

Chris eyed David nervously then said as calm as he could manage, "He said he would go along."

Relief washed through the room from the stances of everyone involved to the rush of breath escaping the girls. Taylor wanted to feel pity towards all involved, but she couldn't muster one ounce. She still had a nagging feeling about her mother, though.

The beautiful blonde stepped forward and leaned down next to David. Her hand brushed lightly against the bandages around his face. "Sweet David, you were too lovely for this world to bear. Please forgive us." Then she blew him a kiss as the others' laughter floated through the room as they headed out the door.

* * * *

Taylor knew the minute she was back in the boiler room

and out of the vision. The putrid smell and the man still holding on to her arm were enough evidence to know that she wasn't safe in her bed. She looked upon the man she now knew as David.

He didn't wear the mask this time and she could see the destruction the fire had left behind. The right side of his face was all that remained as it once was, handsome and smooth. The left side was terribly scarred with jagged ridges and deep gouges of skin missing. Only half of his ear remained. His eyes stared back at her, watching as she assessed all the damage done that disastrous night.

"You understand, don't you?" A slight nod followed his whispered words.

"They weren't innocent." She placed her hand over the one that still held on to her arm. "The boys?"

"They died first ... a long time ago." He pulled his hand from hers.

"And my mother?" Taylor didn't know if she really wanted to hear that he had killed her mom and dad, but something in her needed an answer.

"I didn't kill her. I guess you could say that fate has its own kind of poetic justice."

Taylor felt her heart lift with that news. Maybe justice had been served in some twisted way, but somehow it made her feel a lot better knowing that her mother and father's deaths were not at the hand of the man her mother had failed to save so long ago.

"And me? How did you know about me back then?" Taylor watched him shrink away from her. He tried to look anywhere but at her, as if he were shy or even ashamed of the things he showed her.

She placed a finger under his chin and brought his eyes back to hers. "What about me, David?" She saw something flash in his eyes then. Maybe it was just the fact that she called him by his name.

"You came to me in a dream once. You were all grown up looking like you are right now." He shifted his weight from one foot to the other. "You spoke to me, then you kissed my forehead and I felt peace. I didn't know what it meant back then, just knew that one day it would come to pass."

"What did I say to you?"

"I'm not sure. That part was always fuzzy. I just know that you lean over me and speak softly in my ear. Then you kiss me. That's it."

He took her hand gently and squeezed it. "There is something else you should know. Maybe it was fate or destiny, whatever you want to call it, but when your mother tried to save me, she stopped because she was afraid of me."

"Afraid of you. Why?" Taylor needed to know everything. To understand.

"I saw in her mind she had a daughter, a daughter like me. With observer dreams."

Taylor shook her head vehemently. "No, that can't be true. I was just a young child back then. Besides I didn't get these dreams until after the accident."

David shook his head. "You don't remember, do you? When you were a child did you ever have feelings of déjà vu? Felt like you were doing stuff that had already been done?"

Taylor nodded slightly and her brow furrowed. "But everybody does, so I dismissed them. So did my mom when I would tell her about those feelings."

"She knew. Her sister had them and she was afraid you did too." David dropped her hand and leaned against the table. "That's why she stopped trying to put the fire out. Somehow, she thought not saving me might stop you from being ridiculed for your special abilities."

Taylor didn't know what to say. Here was a man she watched murder nine women and all she felt was remorse for the boy he once was, for the man he could have been. Her mother knew she had these abilities and never told her. Life could have turned out so different for both of them, if only everyone hadn't been so afraid of the unknown.

* * * *

Cade couldn't believe it. It sounded like Taylor was talking calmly with a man. It couldn't be the killer. She'd be scared or crying, screaming, fighting to get away ... something?

Maybe she's playing him. Making him think she's on his side. Yeah, she's a smart woman. Taylor could be charming him into trusting her.

Cade exchanged a look with the other detective and they formulated a plan of attack without speaking a word. The other detective would kick in the door, Cade would rush in first, guns drawn and they would rescue Taylor. If the killer had to go down for her to be saved they were both in silent agreement that it was okay.

He watched as the older officer kicked with all his might. The wood splintered and small shards of wood flew in different directions. Cade aimed his gun in front of him and jumped over the threshold. The other officer was right on his tail.

Cade saw Taylor turn towards the sound of the door exploding. He watched in slow motion as a man grabbed a knife off the table and held it to Taylor's throat. The man was gripping Taylor to him, using her as a human shield. Cade wanted to fire, but knew he didn't have a clear shot and he wouldn't risk hitting Taylor.

Taylor was frightened as the sound of breaking wood resounded throughout the small room. David flinched beside her. When she saw Cade and what could only be another officer standing before her with guns drawn, a small tingle of relief flowed through her. But it was short-lived.

She felt the cold tip of the knife held to her throat. David breathed rapidly in her ear, his arm bruising as he held her tight against him. She had thought she was safe from David, but his insanity had gone too far.

"Freeze! Police! Let the girl go. It's over." Cade looked like he could tear David's heart out with his bare hands, but he managed to keep the anger out of his voice. Taylor saw a cop standing before her, not a man she had recently shared a bed with.

"Taylor, are you all right?" Cade's voice was strained.

Her first instinct was to nod, but the feel of steel against her pulsating artery told her movement was not a good idea. "I'm fine."

"She's coming with me." Taylor felt David's hot breath against her neck. She noticed Cade and the other officer stiffen.

Taylor could see that the situation could turn very ugly very quickly. "David, please. Let them help you. You need help to get over what was done to you. Just tell them and they will fix everything."

She didn't know why she was compelled to help someone who had done such terrible acts, but she didn't want to see any more death. Especially knowing what she knew now.

"You're just like them. You want to condemn me for who I am."

There was something in David's voice. Like it wasn't the

David she had been talking to right before the door was kicked in. She remembered the hostility he had aimed at her the time she had been inside his head.

Could David possibly have multiple personality disorder?

"David, please. You know me. I'm on your side."

"Taylor, do you remember that day in my living room?" Cade's soft-spoken words reached her.

Taylor felt David freeze behind her. The knife pressed harder against her throat and she felt something warm slowly trickling down her neck.

"Cade, I can't let you hurt him." Taylor tried to make Cade understand with her eyes. She knew he wanted her to break the hold David had on her so he could have a shot at taking him down. But there was too much risk to everyone involved if she tried that.

"Taylor, do it!"

She wasn't aware of where the feeling came from, but without warning she was overwhelmed by years of being told what to do. Her mother always treated her like she should be coddled and taken care of. Lana was the same way. Always acting like she was incapable of taking care of herself. She was almost twenty-five years old, far from being a child, and yet here was one more person trying to tell her what to do.

A rational part of her screamed for her to listen to Cade. He was a police officer; he knew what he was doing. Yet she chose to listen to the part of her brain that said she could get herself out of this situation. She didn't need Cade. She didn't need anyone.

"David, put the knife down."

"I can't do that, bitch!"

She knew when he called her that vulgar name that she was no longer talking to David. This was someone else, the evil she knew lurked inside of him.

"Where is David?"

"Taylor, what the hell are you doing?" Cade looked at her like she had just sprouted wings and stated she was preparing for take off. She noticed the other officer sliding slowly off to the side, keeping his gun trained on her and David.

Taylor ignored Cade and tried again. "I want to speak with David." The hand holding the knife to her throat appeared to ease slightly.

"Taylor?"

The muttered word of confusion filled her heart. "It's me, David. I need you to put the knife down, okay? No one's going to hurt you."

"He wants to kill me. I can feel it." She felt the fear from David at the prospect of dying. Even after all he had been through he was still afraid of death.

"I know you feel it. He's just doing his job. Please put down the knife so they won't hurt you. It's over, David."

"If I die, you die too." The evil was back. Taylor knew in her heart that she had to do what Cade had asked. David wasn't strong enough to hold back the evil inside.

She looked at Cade and tried to convey to him with her eyes that she would do what he wanted. The knife slipped from under her neck, she saw the slightest bit of light in the room glint off the blade as it made its way downward towards her chest. Not giving a second thought to her movements, she stomped on David's foot then slammed her head back into his nose. Taylor heard the bone splinter and felt the back of her head become wet.

She jumped away from David. He lunged for her calling her a bitch and a few other choice words. The knife grazed her arm, tearing her shirt. Gunshots rang out. Smoked filled the air. Taylor hadn't even realized she had closed her eyes till she heard Cade begging her to open them.

"Taylor, are you all right?" She heard the concern in his voice.

The other officer was talking into his radio, calling for backup and an ambulance. He gave their location to the person on the other end. She noticed the officer kept his gun trained on David. He was down on the ground, his face covered in blood and his shirt was soaked as well. He was quiet and still, and for the briefest moment she thought he was dead.

The officer had kicked the knife out of his hands and far out of his reach. Helping her to sit up, Cade examined her arm. When he touched the cut she flinched. Blood trickled down her arm, but she couldn't seem to take her eyes from the man who caused her injury. Was it David lying there bleeding to death or was it the wickedness that lived inside him?

"Taylor."

She knew the moment she heard her name spoken in his raspy voice that it was David. She tried to crawl away from Cade, but he refused to release her.

"No, there's nothing you can do for him now." Cade stared her down, once again talking to her like she was some child.

"I have to go to him."

"No, he's dangerous." Cade's eyes narrowed in anger.

"He needs me. Now let me go." Taylor wrenched herself free from Cade's grip and slowly crawled to David.

"Keep an eye on him, Truman, if he moves wrong, shoot him."

Taylor glared back at Cade over her shoulder.

When she reached his side, she knew that it was already

too late. Any ambulance sent might as well be called back and the coroner sent instead. He'd lost so much blood. Between the gunshots and his broken nose, she didn't think there was any way for David to make it out of this room alive. His skin had paled. Even the deep red of his scars was fading to light pink.

"David, I'm so sorry. I didn't want any of this to happen." Taylor brushed his hair back off his forehead.

"Please forgive me, Taylor. I would never have hurt you. Please forgive me." His whispered plea was tinged with a slight gurgling noise. Taylor figured he was choking on his own blood.

Leaning down, Taylor said softly in his ear, "I forgive you for everything. You are avenged and can let go now." As she kissed his brow she saw his face muscles relax and a small smile crease his lips as he slipped from this world into the next. Her heart broke when she finally put together what just happened with what he told her earlier of his premonition of her so long ago. He had dreamt of his own death and hadn't even realized it.

She grabbed both of his hands and laid them across his chest. Her fingertips brushed gently against his eyelids to close his eyes forever.

The tears slipped from under her closed lids as she felt the world swim around her and everything went black.

Chapter Thirteen

The smell of disinfectant and other cleaners reached her nose. She tried to move, to sit up, but her head swam causing nausea to assail her. Taylor reached out blindly. The light pricked her eyelids sending piercing pain straight to her brain.

"Taylor, it's all right. Don't try to move, honey."

Lana's voice was soft and reassuring. Taylor felt the peace and security that her sister's voice always brought instantly fill her heart. She squeezed her eyes tight then slowly opened her eyes a sliver, trying to focus on Lana.

Lana sat in a chair next to the bed and was caressing the back of her hand. She looked haggard, like she hadn't slept in days. Taylor arduously glanced around only to cause more shooting pain to sear through her head so she immediately closed her eyes and heaved a big sigh.

"Where am I? What happened?"

"You were hit by a drunk driver. You're in the hospital." Taylor heard Lana sniff softly. "You've been in a coma for a few weeks."

Taylor's eyes flew open then, not caring about the pain. "What?!"

No way. No way was everything a dream. She couldn't have made up such stuff.

"The doctor says you'll be fine. Other than a broken wrist and a few bruises and cuts, you're fine."

Lana stood now, trying to make Taylor lay back against the pillows. She could not believe it. When the door to her room opened Richard came in with a man at his side.

Cade!

But if she had dreamt the whole thing, if it wasn't real, how could Cade be here? He was a figment of her imagination. Wasn't he?

"Richard, can you help me?" Lana glanced over her shoulder at the two men who had just entered her room.

When he came around to the side of her bed opposite Lana, Taylor looked him up and down. She didn't know what she was looking for until she looked over at her sister and noticed that she wasn't wearing her necklace. No engagement ring graced her sister's ring finger either.

Looking over at Cade, she realized that he looked at her like he didn't know her. Like they had never been intimate. Never fallen in love.

She allowed herself to relax back against her bed and closed her eyes against the rush of searing pain to her heart. Her heart was being ripped out of her chest. It had all been a dream. The killings. Cade's lovemaking. Everything.

"What happened?"

Taylor heard the chair beside her squeak, and then felt Lana's hand grip hers tight. "I don't know. I told her what happened and she flipped out on me. She tried to get out of bed. That's when you guys came in."

A heavy, warm hand felt across her forehead and then came to rest upon her cheek. "It's okay, Taylor. We caught the guy who hit you. He hit another car and spun out into a light pole a few blocks away.

"There's a detective here who needs to ask you a few questions, if you're up to it."

Taylor opened her eyes to see Richard staring down at her. His eyes shone bright with unshed tears. He blinked rapidly trying to dispel them. She glanced over at the man she had thought herself in love with. He had a notepad in his hand.

"I'm fine now. I was just ... shocked is all." Taylor kept her eyes on the man before her, not wanting to look away. She drank him in. His brown hair, his beautiful blue-green eyes. Everything was as she had dreamed.

"This is Detective Cadence Wilson. He's been assigned to your case."

Cadence Wilson. That was a little too weird for comfort.

"Could I have a moment alone with Ms. Cole?" His voice was just like in her dream. Her heart melted.

Lana seemed a little reluctant to let go, but she slid her hand out from Taylor's grasp and walked out the door Richard held open. Before Richard left, Taylor watched as a custodian walked by pushing a cart full of towels. Her heart rate sped up and she knew she might just pass out right there.

The orderly's face was severely scarred. He wore green scrubs and what showed of his arms was scarred as well. He looked in her room and smiled at her, then winked. As the door closed behind Richard, the room spun out of control. Her head pounded with the rush of blood and she felt her stomach clench. Grabbing the rail of her bed she leaned over and puked.

* * * *

Cade watched as the nurse and Lana cleaned Taylor up. It had killed him to step back out of the way after she had thrown up in her sleep. The doctor said he could see no reason why she hadn't woken up. She didn't have a concussion; she'd merely passed out back at the boiler room.

He still couldn't believe that she had caressed the killer as he lay dying. She talked to him and kissed his brow like they were old friends. He desperately needed to find out what happened in that room before Truman busted the door down.

Taylor needed twenty-two stitches to close up the wound on her arm. Unbeknownst to him a bullet had grazed her leg as she tried to get out of the way. That wound took five stitches. Her doctor claimed that she probably passed out because of the blood loss mixed with the trauma of the whole ordeal. But that still didn't explain why she wouldn't wake up.

Lana had screamed long and loud at him about how it was his fault for not protecting her sister. After her tirade she fell into his arms sobbing that she couldn't lose Taylor. He wanted to cry right along with her, but Richard removed her from his arms and held her close till she quieted down.

They all took turns keeping watch over Taylor for the past three days. Cade had to give his statement of what happened to Internal Affairs to make sure it was a clean shooting. The conclusion was that they had no choice but to shoot the suspect.

Trying to sleep in his bed without Taylor in it had proven useless. It was hard to even breathe until he knew she'd be okay. He found himself nodding off more than once sitting in the chair beside her bed, holding on to her hand. He came to the conclusion that he would ask Taylor to marry him the minute she woke up, and even bought a beautiful one carat Marquis cut diamond ring.

Standing there watching Taylor made him feel helpless and he hated that feeling. He felt that way the day his brother and best friend died. He felt that way when he watched their bodies being lowered into the ground and he felt that way when he watched the Night Stalker hold a knife to Taylor's throat. Cade refused to let himself feel helpless anymore.

"Lana?"

He swore his heart stopped beating the moment he heard Taylor call Lana's name. Everybody's movement stopped. The nurse and Lana stared down at Taylor and Cade stood there with his mouth hanging open like an imbecile.

"What's going on? Am I still dreaming?"

"Still dreaming?" Lana clenched Taylor's hand and looked towards Cade with questioning eyes.

Taylor followed her gaze. "Detective Wilson, I'm sorry I must have passed out again."

"Detective Wilson?" Cade reached the bed in two long strides. He could see the confusion written all over Taylor's face as she looked around the room. Stopping to stare at Richard, the nurse, Lana and finally coming to rest back on him.

"Get the doctor. Something's wrong with her." Lana looked upon Richard with worried eyes.

The nurse moved back from the bed and let Cade take her place. She slipped silently from the room, no doubt on her way to retrieve the doctor.

Taylor gripped Lana's hand and scooted away from Cade. She wrapped an arm around Lana's midsection, her eyes filled with tears and she watched him with such trepidation it almost broke his heart.

"I ... I can't tell what's real anymore, Lana. Did I get hit by a car?"

"Yes, honey, but that was months ago. You passed out. The doctor said from stress and blood loss." Cade exchanged a questioning look with Lana before she continued. "The doctor says you should make a full recovery though."

"Are you Cade? Is this real?" Taylor paused in her questioning to look towards Richard. "Was David real?"

Cade reached for Taylor's hand but she withdrew her hand quickly. Gripping the railing instead he answered, "David was real. I'm real. We're all real and we need some answers, Taylor!" Cade couldn't help the anger that flowed from him. *What the hell was going on?*

Everyone in the room flinched at the bite in Cade's words. The minute Taylor hid her head in Lana's stomach he knew he'd been too harsh. Something was wrong with Taylor, she couldn't seem to remember what happened or him for that matter and his nerves were about shot. Before he went and did or said something he might not be able to take back, he headed for the door.

He was determined to just walk out and come back when he was cooler, calmer, but when he looked back he saw Taylor glancing around Lana's side. The fear in her eyes and the tension in the room were almost palpable.

Fear gripped his heart and he nearly choked thinking that he might never get *his* Taylor back.

* * * *

Four weeks had passed since that day in the hospital. Four long, exhausting weeks. Taylor explained to Lana everything that happened. About David and what he had shown her. About their mother being the house mother for Alpha Gamma Delta. Even about the dream of her in the hospital waking after being run down by the drunk driver.

Lana helped her to sort everything out. The murders were real. Cade and Officer Truman killed David. She even pointed out to Taylor she was too young to remember that their mother had worked every couple of weekends as house mother for the sorority to give her friend a weekend off.

Cade sent flowers every day at first, then slowly they tapered off to once or twice a week. Taylor kicked Lana out of the apartment after making her understand she needed some time alone to sort through everything that had happened and to see if she would be able to make it on her own when Richard and she married. She picked up the phone several times a day wanting to call Cade, desperately wanting to tell him why she was afraid of him that day, wanting to tell him how much she missed him. But something held her back.

Maybe it was the fact that she didn't want to exchange one caretaker for another. Maybe she didn't know if her love for Cade was returned. She knew that she had grown stronger over the past couple of weeks. She found a listing on the internet for a psychic with powers similar to hers. After corresponding back and forth through emails and telephone calls, Taylor felt she was finally learning to control her powers. Madame Sylvia had been extremely helpful in teaching Taylor how to control the visions instead of letting them control her.

Lana said Cade asked about her all the time, constantly bugging Richard for updates on her progress. At times it almost seemed like Lana liked Cade, even cared that he was hurting. Lana urged Taylor several times to go and see him, but Taylor's courage ran low by the time she got to the curb outside the apartment. She sent notes through Lana about how she was doing and explaining that she needed just a little more time. She was scared of rejection, scared that maybe what they had was just the spur of the moment attraction, not something lasting.

Consuela moved out, thanking Taylor on her way out with the last load of boxes for catching the *psycho* who had murdered her sister. Although Taylor had been upset by her choice of words, she didn't have the heart to tell her why her sister was targeted by David. Some things were better left unsaid.

Madame Sylvia advised her to keep a running journal of her feelings and any dreams, observer or regular. She still had trouble getting to sleep, sometimes seeing David's face the way it had been so long ago, other times seeing him with the scars and the evil behind them calling her foul names and raising a knife above her ready to strike.

It had taken a lot for her to get to this point in her life, but she finally felt like she was in control. Of her dreams, of her life. It was time to deal with the other unanswered question in her life. Cade.

He was always in the back of her mind niggling at her, causing her to heat to burning at odd moments of the day. She knew in her heart that she had to face him and tell him her feelings, explain everything and see if he still wanted to be with her.

She chose a pretty pink kerchief pattern skirt, a white, low-cut top that showed off just the right amount of cleavage, a denim jacket, her pink suede, lace-up, knee-high boots and a beautiful pink opal choker necklace. She put on a small amount of makeup and made sure her hair passed for presentable.

She called the station only to learn Cade was off sick today. By the time the taxi arrived in front of Cade's driveway, Taylor was worked into a frenzy wondering what was wrong with him, if it was something serious. She rang the doorbell and waited impatiently, hopping from foot to foot, trying to look into the window beside the door to see if she could make out any movement.

When the door finally swung open she got her first

glimpse of Cade in four weeks. His hair was a mess, sticking up and in desperate need of a comb. He wore a pair of old sweats slung low on his hips. His feet and chest were bare. Her hands itched to touch him, but the anger she saw in his eyes stopped her cold.

Before she could even utter the words she had come to say he held up his hand. "Don't say a word."

"But I..."

"I said don't speak. How could you just blow me off like that? How could you throw away everything we had, then just show up like nothing has happened between us? Do you know what I've been going through the past couple of weeks?" He jabbed his finger in her direction, slicing through the air like he was trying to cut the tension between them.

"I've been grilled by Internal Affairs, by my friends, by your sister for God's sake. My family thinks I've lost my mind. Hell, I think I have too. To want you even after I saw you kissing that lunatic who haunted your dreams and hurt your sister. How am I supposed to get on with my life if you think you can just show up on my doorstep looking like that?"

When he finally ran out of steam, she smiled and said, "Do you want me to answer that or am I still not able to speak?"

His look told her he was pretty close to reaching out and strangling her, so she cut the sarcasm and jumped in with both feet and her eyes wide open.

"Things were a bit confusing and crazy when I first woke up in the hospital. Lana helped me work through some things, and to tell the truth I needed to work through some things on my own."

Cade leaned his head against the corner of the door and

closed his eyes. "I called. I sent flowers. Lana told me not to come by until you were ready, but you never called me, just sent short notes stating that you were okay and needed time. I ... what was I supposed to think?"

"I'm sorry I pushed you away. It's just it was all so confusing and I wasn't sure if you loved me the way I loved you. If you could love me that way. I needed to be sure of my feelings for you. If they were even real." Taylor moved slowly towards the doorway hoping he wouldn't slam it in her face while she babbled.

He looked up at her when she ran her hand across his chest. The muscles bulged and flexed underneath her palm. "I've missed you, Cade. Can't we please start again?"

His eyes filled with tears as he grabbed her tight to his chest. Her arms wrapped around him and they both cried. Cade kissed her forehead, moving to her cheek and finally reaching the place she most wanted to feel his lips at that moment. On a moan he deepened the kiss, diving into the recesses of her mouth, his tongue spearing hers.

Taylor felt him moving her inside then heard the door slam behind her. His hands were everywhere, grasping and caressing. She felt him slipping her jacket off, then his hand slid under the hem of her shirt. She felt the fire start to burn low in her belly moving at a fast rate down to her nether lips.

She didn't remember removing her lips from his so he could pull her shirt over her head, but suddenly she was bare from the waist up. The cool air blew across her nipples, revealing that he somehow removed her bra as well. Her breasts ached for his touch, budding tightly just for him. His mouth consumed first one areola then the other.

Her hands moved to the waistband of his sweats sneaking

inside, needing to feel his hot flesh against hers. Taylor grasped his rock solid erection and pumped slowly. He moaned against her breast. Taylor felt him moving her across the room and when the back of her knees hit the sofa she fell upon it taking Cade with her.

He caught himself before he fell completely on top of her. Bracing himself on his elbows he kissed her slow and long. Savoring every lick of his tongue, every nip of his teeth. Taylor reached for him, arching her back her body begged to be entered. She felt him yank her skirt up and a thick finger moved her panties aside, diving deep into her weeping pussy.

"Yes!"

"God, I love you." He breathed into her neck. "Don't you ever go away from me again, Taylor."

"Never again, baby. Never again." Taylor clawed at his back when he removed his finger and positioned his burning flesh at her entrance. She whispered the only word she could think of, "Please."

He pushed in hard and fast. Stretching her. Filling her. They both cried out from the pure pleasure of it. Four long weeks without Cade touching her, filling her, had been pure torture. Now having him was exquisite, and she didn't plan to ever let him go.

They climaxed at the same time, each calling out the others name. Tears filled both their eyes. Taylor pulled Cade down, forcing him to let her take his weight. He felt so good, flesh to flesh.

"I had planned to ask you in a more romantic way, but I don't know if I can wait any longer." Cade pulled back to look her in the eye. His gaze was serious and she stiffened slightly at his tone.

"Okay. What is it?"

"Will you, Taylor Cole, do me the grandest honor of becoming my wife?"

Taylor felt her heart lift and soar through the clouds. She smiled, then screamed out the only answer she could, "Yes!"

He hugged her to him, kissing her neck and then he laughed. Taylor laughed with him, expelling all the tension, confusion and stress that she had been straining against for the past couple months.

She would be okay.

They would be okay.

* * * *

The day was perfect. The sun was shining bright. A slight breeze was blowing helping to make the eighty-five degree whether not so stifling. Her dress blew behind her as she watched her husband cross the dance floor that was constructed outside the reception hall. He grabbed a pink rose off a nearby table's centerpiece. When Cade reached her side he bowed and presented the flower to her.

Taylor curtsied then accepted the rose. "Thank you, kind sir."

"Now if everyone could clear the floor, we would like the brides and grooms to take the floor for their first dance as husband and wife."

Taylor looked across the floor and saw Richard pick Lana up and carry her to the dance floor. She felt Cade's arms lift her as well. When they were finally planted on their feet in the middle of the dance floor, Lana hugged Taylor and then took Richard in her arms as the music started to play. The words to Shania Twain's love song "From This Moment On" floated on the wind.

Taylor and Lana had picked it to be their wedding song because the words seem to fit. With everything that had happened to them over the past year, Taylor felt that life for them was truly beginning with the men they loved. They decided to have a double ceremony when Taylor let it slip to Lana that she was pregnant.

Lana wasn't about to let her baby sister wait to get married when she was showing. It seemed that the moment of passion of getting back together had clouded their judgment and Cade forgot to use a condom. But Taylor didn't care. She was ready to be a mother and Cade was completely ecstatic. After he got over the shock of it.

Now dancing before all their friends and family, both her and Lana twirling in their beautiful wedding dresses, she couldn't be happier. She hadn't had any observer dreams that were serious. A few minor incidents, but nothing as tragic or terrifying as the Night Stalker case.

Seeing Cade now in his black tuxedo, dancing so close to him that you couldn't slip a piece of paper between them, she knew that life truly would be blessed from this moment on. After dancing several more dances and being passed around to Cade's brothers and other family members, they settled at the table to cut the cake.

The cake was a gorgeous three tier chocolate cake covered in white icing. Two statues stood on top, a bride and groom staring into each other's eyes with looks of complete and utter love. They cut the cake and after feeding each other a small sliver, Taylor felt she would implode with all the love she felt in her heart.

"I never would have dreamed I could be this happy." Taylor kissed Cade softly.

Richard pretended to gasp and grab his chest, "What, you mean you didn't *see* it coming?"

Cade laughed out loud, then seeing the sour expression on Taylor's face he sobered quickly. "Man, I hope your kids are funnier than you." He smiled brightly.

Richard lightly punched Cade's shoulder and fired back, "Yeah, well at least my kids won't be floating above my bed at night."

Cade stopped smiling and looked aghast at Taylor. "They won't be able to do that, right?"

Taylor couldn't help it. He was so adorable and completely hers. She rubbed her still flat stomach and laughed as his eyes flew to stare at her belly as she caressed it. "You never know, honey. You never know."

The End

Printed in the United States
60108LVS00007B/178-207

9 781586 087456